Chance Worth Taking

Chance Worth Taking

Lorinda Faye

LFP Publishing

Published in eBook and print by Lorinda Faye, LFP Publishing LLC.
First edition: November 2025

The publisher is not responsible for websites (or other content) that are not owned by the publisher.

ISBN: 979-8-9929051-3-7 (trade paperback), 979-8-9929051-4-4(eBook)

Printed in USA

To every soul who believes in second chances. The kind you give yourself when no one else does. This one is for you!

1

Emily

I feel weight sink into the seat next to me as I stare out at the fast-moving terrain. My eyes stay fixed on the blur outside the window. I let out a small, quiet sigh and then I refold the piece of paper that is in my hand. I put it back into the heart-shaped locket that is hanging around my neck. I tucked it back into my shirt to keep it safe. Then I brace myself, already irritated for what comes next. For the third time...

Why can't these people pick anywhere else to sit? There's a half-empty bus to pick from.

I smell her scent even before I turn my head; musty, sharp, heavy with garlic. My stomach twists. Lately smells bother me. Her silence didn't last long before her words came tumbling out.

"Boy or Girl?"

I turn to her and smile, fake and small before I say *boy.* Then I turned back to the window. Back to my own privacy.

"What are you going to name him dear?"

I roll my eyes because this old lady is clearly not taking the hint to buzz off. She is the third person to ask me a question about the baby since I have been on this stupid bus.

Jesus, doesn't anybody mind their own business?

My head is now pressed against the cool window. My cheek is cold. Based on my body language, if someone were to actually read my body language, it would appear to them that I am not interested in small talk. None at all. I am not interested in a travel companion, or a friend, or anything else considered *friendly*. My body language suggests that I want to be left alone.

But these people feel the need to ask anyway.

They meddle.

They invade.

They disturb.

They are nosy as hell.

And for what? Do they really expect me to give them an honest answer?

I know they have no way of knowing. How could they? I've been told I look older. They see a young pregnant woman and they probably think the best-case scenario. A baby is a blessing. A gift from God. All warm and fuzzy and the little pitter patters and all. Why would they think any differently? Aside from me being alone. But perhaps me being alone is why they are taking such an interest. Still, I don't like it.

I know they have good intentions, but what would they think if I told them the truth? If I didn't lie or embellish at all. I'm not sure there is anyone on this earth that could handle the truth. Hell, I don't know how I am going to handle the truth.

Chance Worth Taking

The truth is... this baby is indeed a boy, and I do not know what I am going to name him. I haven't thought about it yet. I haven't thought about it yet because he isn't my baby. He's someone else's baby. A baby that I got on this bus with and technically stole.

Yes, smelly old lady, I took him without permission.
Yes, I know, I kidnapped him!
Yes, I could go to jail.

I have had enough time now on this bus to imagine all of their confused and surprised faces if they were to hear those words come out of my mouth. Their shock. I picture their jaws dropping. Their disbelieved looks. *The gasps!* Then the panic about what to do with this horrifying information. Do they call the police? Report my crime? Am I even committing a crime? Will someone turn me into some sort of child custody service? Will I be held somewhere until this baby is born? What would they do with this incriminating information? What would these people think of me then, and who would they tell?

How would I expect anyone to respond? This shocking and horrifying information. I am pregnant and I have been on this bus for seven hours now, running away with a baby I stole. One that is not outside of my body like normal people steal babies, but instead I am stealing him *while* he is growing inside my body. And everyone that sits down next to me is so God damn nosy about it. Why do people have to be so God damn nosy?

I'm over it.
I'm over it.
I'm over it.
Oh my God...what have I done?
I face the old lady again.

"I'm not sure yet."

I turn back to the window and press my cheek back to the cold.

2

Emily

I stepped off the bus after nine exceedingly long hours. My back hurt and I was hungry. I didn't have much of a plan. All I had was this piece of paper with an address on it from my momma's locket and her very small suitcase. A faded memory comes to mind.

"I'm hiding this in here Bug. Don't forget about it."

I remember she had both of her hands cupped around my tiny shoulders as she looked me straight in the eyes. She had just hidden the suitcase in my closet behind all of my stuffed animals and toys I didn't play with anymore.

"You might need it someday. Someday you might need to go. If you do, remember this suitcase. Remember the locket. Do you understand me Bug? Do you?"

I remember telling her I won't forget. And I didn't. I checked on it every single night after she died. Every night I made sure it was still in there. I knew then that it was important. Even at four years old. I just didn't know why, until now.

I had wanted so desperately to wear her locket. Sometimes when my father wasn't home, I took it out of the pocket and put it on, or I just held it in my hand. I wanted so desperately to feel closer to her. The locket worked for a short period of time, but those moments, they didn't last long. I knew if my father saw it, he would take it from me, and I would be crushed. Momma said it was important. So I did what she said, and I kept it hidden almost all the time.

It turned out I did need the suitcase someday. I needed it today. Today was the last day I had to pull it out of the closet unused, the locket still zipped up in the inside pocket. Tucked neatly inside of it was a tiny piece of paper with a South Carolina address on it. A piece of paper I've read so many times that I memorized it. A place when I looked it up, appeared to be out in the middle of nowhere.

I don't know why my momma had this address hidden away in her locket. My father told me she was from Ohio. I don't know what this place means to her. Why South Carolina? Why not Ohio? Regardless, it's all that I had at this moment and I was grateful for it.

I remember her wearing this locket, I also remember when she stopped wearing it, which was just before she died. It always looked so pretty on her. Why she took it off? I don't think I'll ever know. But I felt like that piece of paper was a gift. A secret message specifically for me. Maybe a gift she didn't know she was giving me. Or maybe she did know. Maybe it was her plan all along. I wouldn't put anything past anyone at this point. I know my momma loved me and I know my father did not.

My phone dings. I know by now they have probably caught on. I reached for it in my pocket and opened the text. It was from Alicia. The text said that I needed to really think this through. I am not making a very smart decision for myself or for the baby.

What she really means is that I am not making a very smart decision for her and Tate.

Another ding comes through and this time it says to name my price. They will pay me whatever I want. They will up their previous offer and they won't tell my father they gave me the extra money. I just have to come back.

I closed out of Alicia's text, and I looked through my older texts and re-read the last one from my father.

"Make sure the house is picked up good tonight and I don't need any lip this time. Shari is coming over tonight and I need to make a good impression. I don't need you scaring her off. When she comes you make yourself invisible. I don't need her to start asking questions about your condition."

Oh yes, my condition...

Like what's been done to me will magically be cured with a pill or medicine.

My condition came with conditions!

My *condition* is your fault!

I replied *okay* to his text over ten hours ago but what I really wanted to write back was: *I always do father. I always do. And she won't have to ask about anything. Because this time I am going to be invisible... for forever.*

The bus driver told me that there were no Ubers in this town. If I wanted to get somewhere I'd have to walk or know someone to get a ride. Which I did not. I pulled up the map on my phone to see where exactly I was. I had done a little research while I was on the bus, and I had made a reservation at the only Bed and Breakfast in the same town as the address on the paper. According to my phone, I had a forty-five-minute walk from the bus stop. Forty-five more minutes and I get to start my life completely over. Just like I've always dreamed about... well almost like I dreamed about. Regardless, I believe with my whole heart that my life is about to change drastically and for the better.

- 8 -

3

Emily

Early this morning, I waited for my father to leave for work before I got my things in order. I packed the suitcase as full as I could. Being that I was seven months pregnant, and I only had one small suitcase, I couldn't bring many of my things with me.

Next, I loaded up my backpack with my sentimental things, food, and water. I didn't have many opportunities to make memories growing up, so I didn't have many things. No souvenirs from any trips, no keepsakes of my own, nothing to remember important dates from. Mostly things from my momma that I had kept hidden from my father. There were a few pictures of her and I, a small wooden box with the letter P on it, and a hair clip with a poppy flower on it. I put the heart locket around my neck, tucked it in my shirt and then I grabbed the money I had stashed under my mattress that Tate and Alicia gave my father for the baby. I took it last night while he was passed out drunk. They had given him thirty thousand dollars so far and there was only twelve thousand dollars left. It was supposed to be my money, not his to spend on whatever he spent it on. My guess would be drugs, alcohol, and women.

Then I called myself an Uber and headed to the bus station. I showed the ticket collector the address and then I bought my ticket. Lucky for me there was a stop in the same town. Which now puts me here on the front steps of the Four-Leaf Clover Bed and Breakfast.

I don't know why I am crying now. Maybe it's just these crazy pregnancy hormones. Or maybe it's because I'm just so damn tired from what felt like a long week. It could be because I haven't eaten much today. Or it could be because now my momma's suitcase has a broken wheel. Whatever the reason is, I am already extremely embarrassed. And I haven't even rang the doorbell.

The lady who took my reservation sounded old. Like a sweet, kind old lady. She made making a reservation easy. I am a little nervous that she will judge me when she sees me. Maybe she will be forgiving of my situation. Hopefully she is modest and will not ask questions. Hopefully, she isn't as nosy as the people on the bus.

I wipe off the tears on my face. I am sure that my eyes are stained red, but I don't have the ability to do anything about it or to really care at this point. I have to get off my feet as soon as possible. I pressed the doorbell and waited. It took a while for someone to open the door. When it does open, it only opens a crack. I cannot bring myself to look up just yet.

"Can I help you?" a man's voice says.

Oh shit! It's not the sweet old lady I talked to on the phone. Now I'm even more embarrassed.

"Yeah, umm... I'm here for a room."

I can't hide the nervousness in my voice.

God why do I have to sound so weak?

"I spoke with a woman earlier. She said she had a room for me that I could rent for a while?"

The door creaked farther open, and I am forced to look up. Standing in front of me is a guy who looks like he is around my age. An incredibly attractive guy.

I can't help but smile at him, but I am caught off guard. I suddenly became self-conscious. *Oh God, I hope I don't look stupid.* I probably look so stupid. I'm standing here in front of him; eyes stained with tears and pregnant. Extremely pregnant. I probably look like I got swept up into a tornado today and then let go, it not wanting me either. I should have dug out my brush when I got off the bus. Why didn't I think about doing that? It's bad enough I am standing here *this* pregnant, I could have at least looked like I was put together a little more.

I watch as his Adams apple bobs up and down. He clears his throat.

"Yeah okay, Lily has retired for the night. She gets up early so I guess you get me as your host tonight. Come in."

He widens the door all the way.

Why is he so cute and why do I have to be standing here looking like I do? This is just my luck. I walk four steps in and turn to watch him shut the door. Then he turns back to me.

"Can I take your suitcase for you?"

He reaches out his hand to take the handle from me.

"Thank you, I sort of broke the wheel on the way here." I reply nervously, now extremely embarrassed by how much of a mess I am.

"That's okay. I got it."

He lowers the handle and picks it up with the side handle with little effort. He steps forward and motions with his free arm for me to follow him.

"We can head upstairs and get you settled into your room."

The house looks so big and old. Good old, not gross old like the houses I am used to seeing. There is a lot of old looking woodwork, big windows, and doors. All polished and clean. The staircase is huge and is made of solid wood with a double railing. The kind you would see in old estate home magazines.

When I was younger, I was obsessed with old historic houses. I used to look through old magazines all the time. Until my father caught me and threw them in the trash, then he told me I'd never live in a house that nice. But still, it's nothing I have ever seen in real life. I have never even lived in a house with a staircase before. It is a little intimidating. Even so, I am in awe.

I follow whoever he is up the stairs.

"I'm Reader by the way." he says as he turns and looks at me still climbing the stairs.

That's an interesting name.

He faces forward again and continues to climb the stairs.

"I guess it was rude of me to not introduce myself. You didn't mention your name."

"It's Emily."

"Well, it's nice to meet you, Emily."

He stops at the first door at the top of the stairs and sets down my suitcase.

"So, you have a choice." he says as he opens the door and motions like Vana White on the show Wheel of Fortune.

"Behind door number one we have the beach room."

He takes a step inside.

Themed rooms. I wasn't expecting that.

I entered the room and looked around. It is definitely beachy. Seashells lined up on shelves and a light blue hue painted on the walls. There were pictures of beaches hung on the walls. It was so pretty. I turned back to look at him but he was already back out into the hallway. I followed him towards door number two.

"This one is the Paris room. Lily had someone come in and paint this huge wall mural of the Eiffel Tower. It's a little much for me but if you are a fan of Paris, I guess it's kind of cool." he says with a casual shrug.

He walks past me back out to the hallway again and down the hall. He motions to the right as I catch up.

"This is the bathroom. It is a shared space but lucky for you, you are the only one here at the moment. So you can have it all to yourself."

He grins back at me and it catches me off guard. He has the most perfect straight white teeth. I can't help feeling a little bit flustered over them.

When we reached the last room, he swung open the door.

"This last room is, well, quite interesting I guess you can say. Lily has a thing for Elvis. I will just let you see for yourself."

I take a couple steps into the room and the first thing I see is a life-sized cardboard cutout of Elvis Presley and the words *Elvis is alive* on the wall next to it.

"Wait, I thought Elvis died?"

"He did, but Lily thinks he's still alive hiding somewhere amongst civilization, not wanting to be found."

He shrugs.

"I can't change her mind. Crazy thing is a lot of people pick this room on purpose. I guess they like the company." he laughs.

"Oh... okay."

"Well, what do you think?" he folds his arms over his chest and waits patiently for my answer.

I am completely in awe of this house. It's a lot different from the trailer I've lived in my whole life.

"Wow, the choices are, well, it's... um... all very cool. It's a hard decision. Yeah... as cool as Elvis is, it's also kind of creepy how he just stares at you. I don't think I could sleep peacefully at night or change my clothes in front of him for that matter." I joke.

He laughs at my joke. I liked how it felt.

"I think I am going to take the beach room; I've never been to the beach before. It might feel like I'm on a little vacation." I say nervously.

Shoot why did I say that? That's too personal. I hope he doesn't ask me where I'm from.

"Where are you from?"

Damn it.

I didn't really prepare for questions.

"Um, just from a small town about nine hours away in West Virginia." I say quickly, trying to cut off the topic.

"That beach room looks amazing and I'm very tired."

I fake yawn hoping he will buy it.

The truth is I slept a lot on the bus so nobody would talk to me. It did not work that well, but I still got some sleep.

"Okay then, excellent choice. Let's get you settled in."

We walked back down the hall to the beach themed room; he grabbed my suitcase that was still in the hall and sat it on the chair in the corner of the room.

He turns and looks at me again. He has my full attention.

"There are fresh towels in the bathroom and everything you will need for a bath or a shower. Just look around. If you need anything else just ask. Lily serves breakfast any time after six am. She's an early bird. But she's more than accommodating. Just let her know. I on the other hand am not an early bird but more of a night owl so if you need anything to eat tonight or any other night you can find me in the kitchen pretty late. Just come on down. The kitchen is just to the left of the stairs, through the dining room. Can I get you anything else?"

He's looking at me attentively. His brown eyes felt like they were burning mine. I blink hard expecting pain. Nothing.

"I think I'm good for now. I'm going to use the restroom then head to bed. It's been a long day."

"Copy that."

I thanked him and he left me in the beach room alone. I look around and take it all in. My momma would love this room. She used to tell me about the beach when she tucked me into bed when I was little, some of those memories faded.

I take a few minutes to unpack my things. Then I shoved my suitcase in my closet. There isn't a lot to unpack but it feels good for a moment just to organize and settle in. I do not know how long I will be here or what my actual plan is, but this is a start, I guess.

Once I got organized, I grabbed a change of clothes and headed to the bathroom. I decided to take a bath and relax. We didn't have a tub at my father's house, so I never got to enjoy one. I walked in and found a huge white claw footed tub. On the shelf next to it were all kinds of bath supplies.

The tub is also like the kind you see in fancy magazines, same as the stairs. I pick up a towel and bring it to my face. It is dark grey and so soft. The softest towel I have ever felt. And it smelled so good. Fresh. It smelled clean. Like lavender. It took me a minute to figure out how to plug the tub. Once I did, I began filling it up with warm water, adding bath salts that smelled amazing and got better as the water filled up. I dripped in a few drops of bath oil, then settled in, the water feeling magical. This was going to be an amazing first bath.

4

Reader

I knew we were getting a new guest tonight, but I didn't know it was going to be a girl my age. A pregnant one at that.

She looked rough. I don't mean that in a bad way, like she isn't pretty. She is very pretty. She just looked like she'd had a few bad days. Tired maybe. Nine hours on a bus would make anybody look like that.

She didn't seem to have a whole lot of things with her. One small suitcase and a backpack. That is probably fine for her but when her baby comes along, it's clear she has nothing for him or her.

I do have a little bit of experience with pregnancy. I am by far not an expert, but I was thirteen when my mother was pregnant with my brother. So, if I can help her in any way, I will.

Lily and I became business partners when my parents passed away almost a year ago. If you can call this a business... the B&B doesn't see a lot of guests. We are just too small of a town. But we both enjoy it, and we make a good team. Lily's been in our home for most of my life. She moved in when her house caught fire. My parents insisted she come in and help them start the B&B. A dream my mother had for most of her adult life. My father could care less, which was why bringing Lily on was perfect. My mother wanted to enrich others' lives here at the B&B and in her books. Lily was the perfect addition. She's proven so again and again, and she's been a part of our family ever since.

Neither of us really needs the income. My parents had money from the sales of their books. Both were highly successful authors. My father published thirty-two novels, and my mother published forty. One of them was released after she passed. So the income has been plentiful and steady for me. Lily made some smart investments after her husband died years ago and is happily living off those. She's only got herself to worry about, and I only have myself, but we are our own kind of family. She is the only person I have close to me. The rest of my biological family, I have a valid feeling that they only care about me because they know how successful my parents were. They haven't been a staple in my life, not ever.

I knew Emily was going to choose the beach room. I saw the way she looked at it when I opened the door. She looked at it with longing. Then she mentioned that she had never been to the beach before. I made a mental note right then to take her to the beach. Every person in this world should see the ocean and to also feel the sand between their toes. My favorite thing about the beach is the smell the salt leaves in the air. I can smell it from miles away. I have so many memories with my mother at the beach and that smell brings them all back. I want to go soon for me too.

Chance Worth Taking

This might sound a bit strange and too soon, but I feel like I can read Emily pretty well. Like I have an instinct for her. An instant closeness. Maybe it's our age, or maybe it's just my own need for companionship and friendship. Since my parents died, I've closed myself off. I didn't need the sympathy. I didn't need those awkward *"how are you's,"* with sad, concerned faces, or *"I'm so sorry Reed, let me know what you need."* And then not one of them actually meaning it. Nobody really means it, except Lily. Lily did and it's been a blessing to have her look after me. I am technically an adult, but just her being the warm kind person she is, she has definitely been the reason I've made it this far without cracking. Her and this Bed and Breakfast.

I feel like Emily and I can connect. Maybe it's too early to call but as of right now, I hear her up in that bathtub probably having the most relaxing moment. I knew when she said she was going to head to bed that she didn't mean it. I knew she was thinking about that tub. I don't know how, but I just knew it.

5

Emily

I must have soaked for an hour. Long enough for most of my body to look like a raisin. Everything but my huge belly was under the water. My belly popping out of the water like a giant white island. I think the baby liked it too because he sure did kick a lot.

I didn't know a bath could feel so good, or fluffy towels, or bath salts. I've never smelled like this or felt my skin this soft. The water really took a lot of pressure off my body. I felt light as a feather for a moment. I almost felt normal again.

I took my time drying my body and my hair with the soft towels. I changed into a comfortable oversized sweatshirt and a pair of sweatpants, then I walked back to my room to brush my hair. After I settled in again, I realized I was still hungry, and I had no water to drink in my room.

I descended the grand staircase in search of the kitchen. It was easy to find. Exactly where Reader said it would be. When I walked in, he was seated on a stool at the counter. I couldn't see what he was doing since his back was to me.

I didn't want to scare him, so I made a soft noise by clearing my throat.

He turned his head in my direction.

"Emily, hey! How was your bath?"

He closes the book he has opened in front of him.

He must have read the embarrassment on my face.

"Sorry, I could hear the water running. Most of the female guests love the tub, so it's common for it to be used on the first day they arrive. Though... it is a little awkward when a couple uses it. I will spare you the details."

He winks at me.

I blush immediately.

Why am I blushing?

"I appreciate that." I replied quickly hoping to stop the blushing.

"Can I get you something? Water? Food? You're hungry, aren't you?"

I shake my head no then hesitate.

"I... don't want to bother you. I was just going to grab some water and maybe some toast to hold me over until breakfast. I didn't realize I was so hungry until now."

He stands up from his stool and motions for me to take a seat.

"Here, please sit."

"That's okay, really I don't want to bother you." I reply feeling uncertain about his hospitality.

He walks over to me, and I immediately feel heat rush through my body just from his closeness. He puts both of his hands on my shoulders and speaks to me quietly. Now my body feels like it's on fire.

"If Lily were to walk in at this moment, she would have my head on a platter that you are in her kitchen, in your condition, and I'm not getting you what you need."

My condition.

I wince at his word choice thinking of my father.

"Now take a seat because I kind of like my head where it is at the moment."

He drops his hands to my forearms and walks me over to the stool, gently pushing me down until I am seated.

Okay then.

That's not awkward.

At all.

"Now you are hungry right? And do not lie." he says with his back now to me as he starts pulling food out of the fridge.

"I don't want you to go to any trouble." I whisper.

But the second I finish getting these words out he is standing in front of me again. This time he's crouched down to my eye level.

"Emily, I don't mind." he says firmly then stands back up and heads to the other side of the counter where he is setting up food.

I am a little surprised by his intensity. I don't know what to say. He's bossy yet nice and persistent. I'm not sure I know how to handle that. And his eyes on mine. They've left me feeling speechless. I can't think of anything else to say. Not one thing.

He continues talking which I find relieving.

"Now I know this isn't the healthiest choice, but for this late at night it is the perfect comfort food. My mother taught me how to make the best grilled cheese, so I hope it hits the spot."

Yum.

"I'm sure it will be perfect, thank you."

He grabs a loaf of bread. It looks like fancy bread. Not the $1.99 plain white generic bread I always get. The kind that costs a lot of money at the grocery store. I have seen it there but have never bought it because we could never afford it. I watch in silence as he grabs a flat pan and turns on the gas stovetop on low.

"The secret is to cook it slowly. If you cook it too fast the bread toasts too quickly and the cheese won't melt to perfection. Then it doesn't taste as good."

He looks up and grins, I imagine it's because he is proud of himself for knowing how to perfect the perfect grilled cheese. Most guys I know don't even cook.

He has a really nice smile.

And perfect teeth. Both of which I keep noticing and keep mentioning in my head.

He has the perfect shade of dark brown hair; it's almost black and dark brown eyes to complement.

I catch myself staring.

He catches me too.

He smiles again, then looks back down to cut thin slices from a block of cheese.

I feel the heat in my face again.

I need to quit doing that!

"This cheese is my absolute favorite. It's Cracker Barrels white sharp cheddar."

He makes a sliced pile of it on the cutting board.

He takes a knife and spreads a thick layer of butter on the outsides of four slices of bread. Then he walks over to the stove and sets those pieces of bread flat on the pan. He grabs the cheese slices and layers those on the pieces of bread and then covers that up with the remaining two pieces of bread.

When he's done assembling the sandwiches, he turns back to the counter and leans down on his elbows facing me.

"How old are you Emily?"

I am slightly embarrassed because I am pregnant.

"Eighteen, almost nineteen."

He lets out a sigh.

"I'm nineteen. It's better than when I was eighteen."

He shakes his head then turns around.

I have no idea what that means.

He walks over to the stove to check on the grilled cheeses.

"What are you reading?" I ask as he's flipping the sandwiches.

His book is laying cover down on the counter next to me so I cannot see what it is. As I reach for it to take a look, he grabs it quickly and sets it over by the stove.

"It's just a book that I found lying around." he fires back looking a little embarrassed.

"Tomorrow I'm going to take a trip to the library and pick something better up."

He walks to a cabinet and pulls out two small plates and sets them on the counter. He turns back to the stove, waits another minute then takes off the grilled cheese's, putting them onto separate plates. He slices them in half diagonally with the spatula and hands me one of the plates. He takes his plate, comes around to the other seat, and sits down next to me.

"Thank you."

I take a small bite and my eyes widen instantly. *Wow!*

"Reader this is amazing!"

The cheese is so creamy, and the bread is toasted perfectly but it's so thick too. I didn't know grilled cheese could taste this good!

"I know right? I make these a lot when I get hungry at night. It's this or a bowl of cereal. I figured I could do you better than a bowl of cereal."

Now he's grinning.

We cleared our plates then Reader loads them into the dishwasher and cleans up the kitchen. He wouldn't let me help. He said Lily would have his head again if she found out he didn't clean up the mess he made.

When he was done, he reached inside the fridge again and pulled out two bottles of water.

"Here, why don't you take these upstairs with you."

I take them from him, say my thank you's and head back up the grand staircase with a full belly and a huge smile on my face.

I think I like it here.

6

Reader

That was the first time I've made a grilled cheese since my parents died. I didn't lie about making them at night, I just hadn't done it in a while. I have been wanting to make one for a while now but haven't been able to until now. I know it's kind of weird, but some memories hurt more than others.

Making it for Emily felt right. It felt good. There's a bunch of other things I can't do yet. Like reading my mother's new book. The one that just hit the shelves four months ago. Her words still feel too fresh. I've read most of my parents' books and I don't have any problems with the other ones. This one... it feels more like a ghost. Because the book is here but she is not.

My mother started throwing her books at me when I was fifteen. She's a romance writer but she doesn't always give it the typical happily ever after ending. Sometimes I find it ironic that her life ended the way it did. Right next to my father in a tragic tale. Their love cut short by a man with a medical emergency. Simple explanation, the wrong place at the wrong time. It was tragic.

Chance Worth Taking

Or was it not so tragic? They died together. Madly in love. Life full of mostly happiness. One of them never had to go on living without the other. I think about this often. I think about the way she wrote and the way she told her stories. Quite different from her life, aside from her death.

Her and my father had a fairy tale life. They both wrote constantly. Right next to each other most of the time. Click, click, click. They never drove each other mad with their constant clicking or writers block when one had it and the other didn't. I used to love just being in their presence when they were together, writing or not. They were a true pair. And they died that way too. Hell, my mother would have probably written their story, with that death, and it would have been completely on brand.

My mother would hand me the books she wanted me to read; in the order she wanted me to read them. I learned a lot about love and feelings. She always sat me down before I was allowed to start reading it and she always said the same thing.

"Now Reed, this is just a story. It's not how all love goes. The parts that make you feel good, those are true, but the parts that don't... that's just there for the story baby. Those things don't happen with love. Those things won't happen to you. They are just for entertainment."

So, I learned that people who are in real love don't set each other on fire, murder each other, cheat, lie, disappear, or whatever twisted tale my mother spun up to make a story great. I learned that real love was an entirely different language all together. A magical one. When I was done reading her books, I would open the notebook I had gotten for my fourteenth birthday and write poems from the feelings I felt in her books. That's the book Emily saw.

I had just finished my fourth poem when my mother found my notebook.

"Reed! These are amazing baby! Are you for real right now?" she'd asked me one night with a shocked look on her face.

She immediately called for my father who ran into the living room thinking something bad had happened but instead found my mother in tears over a poem I wrote. Nothing was private in our family, and I guess that was okay. My parents treated me like a writer, and we shared everything we wrote with each other from that day forward. Except this new book... but I can't bring myself to read it just yet.

Emily's sandwich was gone before I could blink, I almost asked her if she wanted another one, but I didn't want to embarrass her. I could sense her timidness and knew that she probably needed to get a bit more comfortable before I went all intense on her demanding that she eats for two and not just like one small mouse.

I also didn't want her to see what I was writing. Not yet. Right now, I just wanted to get to know her. That's why I will invite her to the library tomorrow. I think she'd really enjoy that. I wanted to see if she liked anything about my world. I wanted to see if we truly did share some sort of instant connection.

7

Emily

I am making my way down the grand staircase again after what was my best night's sleep ever. That mattress was the most comfortable thing I've ever slept on, and I didn't have my father or his temper on my mind. I just had me, the baby, a little bit of Reader, and my new life.

The strong aroma of freshly brewed coffee hits my nose before I am even halfway down the stairs. It smells so nice.

The baby's doctor told me that I can have one cup a day. Back home we did not have enough money for coffee so when I am able to enjoy a cup, it's something I really look forward to.

I see who must be Lily, hunched over the stove. She looks like she is stirring a pot of something that smells as delicious as the coffee does. She's humming to soft music that is playing in the background.

"Good morning" I call out.

Lily turns quickly. "Oh, hello darling."

She gives me a wide smile which makes me feel welcome.

"I am so glad you were able to make it in last night. I hope Reed was a sufficient host. I sure do get tired early these days. So, I apologize I could not wait up. Now what can I get you for breakfast? I see you are with child dear. How about some old-fashioned oats and fruit?"

I am with child. Ouch… that's embarrassing.

I need to stop being so embarrassed. None of this was my fault. Not really.

I took a seat in the same spot Reader or *Reed* kindly put me in last night.

"Oh yes, thank you so much. That would be wonderful."

I'm not as shy with her…

"Do you drink coffee dear?"

"Yes please. A small cup with cream and sugar if you don't mind. I can get up and grab…"

But before I could even think about standing up, she interrupts me.

"No, no you sit. Let me get it for you. It has been a while since I've had someone like you in my home so please let me dote on you a bit."

Like me?

She sets the coffee mug down in front of me with a warm smile. She looks like she is in her mid-seventies. Maybe older. She's warm and round and everything I pictured a kind old lady to look like.

"You have exceptionally beautiful green eyes my dear. More hazel though. My daughter had green eyes. She used to get anything she wanted with those eyes. Got her into a lot of trouble. Especially with the boys." she said as she stirred in the sugar and turned back to the stove.

That felt a little bit sad for a moment, making me miss my mother and then I felt embarrassed, again. I can just imagine what she thinks of me being pregnant. I shake it off.

"What are you cooking may I ask? It smells amazing."

"This dear is supper. It is my grandmother's famous family recipe. Chicken and dumpling soup. I always make it the day a new guest arrives. It's become tradition. Reed looks forward to it as well since I only make it occasionally. He will probably thank you for it when he gets up. How old are you dear? You look to be about the same age as Reed?"

"I am eighteen ma'am. Almost nineteen."

"I see and you are already with child. Just like my daughter was."

Oh...

I didn't know what to say so I just stayed quiet.

After a long pause she says.

"Well, you both are welcome here for as long as you need." she smiles again at me.

"It's been a long time since there's been a baby in this house so, if need be, you are both welcome to stay."

"Thank you, ma'am. I... uh we appreciate that."

"Please just call me Lily. Now let's get you and that baby some breakfast."

Lily made me real oatmeal on the stove. I looked around for a microwave thinking maybe she didn't have one. But there was a small one on a stand in the corner. She really is old-fashioned. I bet she makes everything from scratch. I've never known what it was like to have a grandmother or much less a momma for very long, so I think I could definitely get used to all of this... I'm not sure what to call it.

Spoiling?

Hospitality?

Just grand mothering?

Whatever it is called. It is new to me, and it feels good. Different from what I am used to, which had become more like a slaving after my alcoholic father and his floosies that I never see... *because I am to be invisible.*

After breakfast Lily gave me a tour of the house and its grounds. She told me that the house used to be a mansion back in 1905 when it was built. Owned by a Carolina government official. She moved in ages ago with Reed and his parents with the dream of opening a Bed and Breakfast. Keeping it to its true construction. The hard woods are original and so is the landscaping design outside.

She took me to the back yard first. It was impressive. There were tons of green bushes trimmed perfectly in the shape of circles and squares. Then for color there were a large amount of rose bushes. Lily told me that they were called Knockout Roses. And they were bright pink and vibrant and bloomed all season long.

Inside, the upstairs was reserved for the guests. Which I had already seen with Reader. Downstairs has the big entry with the grand staircase, the large kitchen, a dining room with seating for twelve, a large living room with a huge fireplace and mantel. On the mantel there were two matching vases or maybe they were urns. I wasn't sure. There were also massive bookshelves on both sides of it, loaded with books.

"Those are Reed's books." she points out.

"He loves to read. Got it from his parents who were both published authors. I had those bookshelves installed for him about six months ago to hold them all. A piece of this house that's just his."

So, his parents were authors. I wonder what happened to them?

We made it to the back side of the house, which she says are her and Reed's rooms and a smaller den she uses for an office.

"These rooms are not for guests for obvious reasons but if you ever need anything just knock. We are always here to help. And that is the tour. Reed gets up sometime late morning. He really needs to shake these teenage years, but the child's been through a lot. The town is close but maybe it's too far of a walk for a woman with child, if you need something you can wait for Reed and he can drive you where you need to go. And that is all I can think of."

We make our way back to the staircase.

"Wow, Lily everything really is so nice, and you are so kind. I do not know how to thank you really."

"Oh dear, no thanks needed."

She rubs the back of my shoulder and walks back to the kitchen.

All right. Now what?

I'm not sure so I headed back up the grand staircase and back into the beach room.

8

Emily

I hear my phone ding as I climb the stairs. I'm certain it is my father. He's finally figured out that I'm not at home and he's probably figured out that I took the money. My money. I don't even want to read the message. Maybe I won't. It doesn't really matter what he says. I'm not going back. And the way I see it, he can't make me. Nobody can make me. Not without them all exposing themselves. I can't imagine for the life of me or this child, why they would want to do that. Ever.

It's very weird being pregnant with someone else's baby. You still feel everything. And although this is the first time I have been pregnant, I couldn't imagine it being much different from being pregnant with my own baby. Other than knowing the baby won't look anything like me and I wouldn't have been keeping this baby. You still develop a love that grows deep. It's grown deeper the farther I have gotten in this pregnancy. I am seven months now, and I feel for this baby what I expect most expecting mothers would feel for their own baby. I feel like we have this special bond between us, a secret I can't tell anyone, and I know now how much in love I am with him, and I haven't even met him yet.

I spent a lot of time in my room back home, I didn't feel loved or safe for that matter, so I am beyond excited to start new somewhere else. A fresh start. I am most excited to finally be free… free of my father and that small lifeless town.

I have enough money to make it here for a while with the money I took. Money that was supposed to be my money. Tate and Alicia were to pay me ten thousand dollars for every trimester of this pregnancy. My father had just gotten paid the week before for the third trimester. Money I never saw. Money that he threatened me over if I told them that he took it instead of giving it to me. The other money he had spent already. I know when he does find out that I took the money, he is going to be angry. Very, very angry. The rest of the deal was that upon delivery I would get ten thousand more. For a total of forty thousand dollars. To us that was a ton of money. What he spent the other eighteen thousand on, I have no idea. But he's not getting the rest of the money now, because I ran. Tate and Alicia had decided the day before I left that they wanted to end the pregnancy. They didn't want the baby anymore. Which is the reason I ran.

So, I had enough money to make it until the baby was born and a little bit after that. But once the baby got older, I would need to find a job and a babysitter. The problem is, I don't know yet if I will be able to stick around in one place. I don't know yet if my father or the baby's biological parents will try to find us. If they will search for us. I don't know what they will do *if* they find us. I hadn't as of now thought that far ahead. I just knew after my last doctor's appointment that I needed to leave, and quickly.

So, it's really one day at a time. I don't even know how I would pay for the birth of this baby and how I would cover any of the medical issues he could possibly have. These are things I should probably have more concern for, but my top priority was getting this baby away from his awful parents and me away from my awful father. I had to get *us* safe.

I decided it would do me good to take a walk through the gardens. I'm not sure how far I'd get, but it was worth a try. And it was beautiful weather in South Carolina in May. Warm. Not too hot for being heavily pregnant.

I headed down to the living room to pick out a book to take with me hoping Reader wouldn't mind. I didn't have many opportunities to read good books where I came from and I love to read. The only library I was exposed to was the school's library and I outgrew those books by the tenth grade.

The bookshelves here were loaded with books. From so many authors. I remember Lilly saying that Readers' parents were both authors but from the number of books here, I don't think I could pick out which ones were their books. I don't even know Readers' last name.

I skim them, suddenly stopping on a book of poems. I take that one off the shelf and head out to the back gardens.

The gardens were elaborate. At least I thought so. I don't have anything to compare them too, except what I've seen in magazines. Every bush was shaped in a perfect circle or square, leading you down multiple paths. Along the paths were the tallest trees I've ever seen. They had to be old because they were so big. At the bottom of the property was a stream with fast flowing water. The sound of it pleasing my ears.

Chance Worth Taking

I picked a spot under one of the trees to sit down and then opened the book of poems. It was a book of love poems.

I began reading but then was hit by a memory. I had to write this poem in my fifth grade English class. It could be about anything, so I wrote it about my momma. It was very simple and immature. I only got a B on it, but I was super proud of it. When I brought it home, my father read it and laughed.

I remember him saying...

"Is this how you remember her?"

He laughed so hard, mocking me. Then he crumbled it up and tossed it in the garbage before he walked away, still laughing at me. After he had fallen asleep that night, I snuck out of my bed and took it out of the garbage, smoothing its wrinkles. Then I stuck it between two pages of a book I had. A book I just realized I left at home.

"The shade feels nice, doesn't it?" Reader's voice startled me.

"Oh... hi."

"I didn't mean to scare you." he smiles.

"Mind if I sit down?"

"Not at all."

He takes a seat next to me, then looks up.

"These trees are Sycamore trees. They can grow to be about a hundred feet. I'm quite sure they have been here since the beginning of time; they look so old."

He's looking up at the sky and smiling. I study his profile. He looks genuinely happy. His brown eyes reflecting the bright sky making them lighter for a moment.

I'm completely caught up in his smile when he asks me how I like the book.

Caught gazing at him, I try to recover quickly.

"Oh, it's good. I was just thinking about this poem I once wrote in English class when I was in the fifth grade. It was not even close to as good as these ones."

I laughed nervously.

"I hope it's okay that I borrowed it?"

"Of course, Emily. I'm glad you like it. Borrow anything you want. So, listen, I was going to head into town. I was thinking maybe you'd like to come along. I can show you around a bit?"

"Oh, okay, yeah that would be nice."

He makes me so nervous. I hope that it isn't that obvious. The thought of spending an afternoon with him almost makes me forget why I'm here in the first place. This is the first time I have been excited to do something new in a long time.

He reaches for my hand and helps me up, which isn't that easy these days.

9

Emily

Our first stop was the library. Inside looked like another historical building. It was huge. Three floors and so many books.

My moment of awe was broken by Reader's voice.

"It's beautiful, isn't it?"

I watch him gaze around the enormous building. It seems like he is taking it in for the first time also, although I know that isn't true.

"Yes." I reply softly not fully convincing myself that I was referring to the library or if I was referring to Reader.

Both things are deserving of this awe moment. I pull myself together.

"I have never seen this many books in one place before. The only library I have ever been in was the school library and I went to a pretty small school. This is, I don't know how to describe it... it's just wow!"

"It is pretty great, isn't it? Follow me." he said as he walks away from me way too quickly.

I follow behind him. He takes me to an aisle that's labeled Poetry.

"Poetry is one of my favorite things to read. It's basically about feelings. Feeling with texture, words with texture, words with color, about anything. You can write poems about trees, people, animals... a place, a thing. Anything really and you can get a very multi-dimensional feeling from it. Most people only associate poetry with love or heartache, but it can express all feelings. Sometimes it is just nice to read a poem and know someone else has felt a certain way about the same thing as well. Maybe you couldn't articulate the words properly, but I bet you could always find a poem about it. It's similar to what music can do for a person. I just prefer poetry verse lyrics. Doesn't make me the most popular kid though."

He shrugs then turns his back not allowing a response from me.

He pulls a few books off the shelves and hands them to me. By the time he is done, I have eight books stacked up in my arms.

"There, that should do it for today." he says with a huge smile.

"Let's go check them out."

I look down at the stack of books in my arms and then laugh.

"Today? I'm supposed to read all these today?"

Reader laughs.

"No Emily. You can take your time. You have two weeks before they are due back."

I am glad he cleared that up.

We walked over to the checkout counter where Reader greets the woman behind the counter.

"Hey Marianne. How have things been?"

"Reader! It's so nice to see you. It's been a little while since you've been in. Are things good? You've been okay?"

"Yeah. I'm good. Just been busy with Lily with the Bed and Breakfast. She's slowing down a bit these days, so I try to stay close and pull my weight."

"Oh, that is good. Please tell her hello. Let her know I am thinking about her, and I will stop up soon for some tea."

"Sure, she would like that." Reader says genuinely.

I've never met anyone as kind as he was before. I find myself in disbelief over it.

"By the way, this is Emily."

He motions over to me standing behind him.

"She is staying at the Four Leaf at the moment."

"Well, hello dear. Aren't you a pretty one! Is this your first time in the Carolina's?" Marianne asks me.

"Yes, ma'am it is. It's incredibly beautiful here. I really like the trees. They are so tall here."

Marianne scans the library books that Reader took from my arms and sets them on the counter. She tosses a receipt inside one of the books then puts the books in a reusable bag.

"Yes, they are. Tallest around. I really hope you enjoy your stay."

"Thank you, Ma'am, I'm sure I will."

Marianne hands Reader the bag and we head back towards the door.

"Everyone is so nice here." I point out as we exit the library.

"It's very...not what I'm used to."

"Yes, for the most part people are generally good here. Do you want to grab a quick lunch?" Reader asks.

"Sure. I could eat."

"Great. We can grab something from across the street."

As we were crossing the street I noticed a small group of people who looked to be our age huddled together on the sidewalk nearby. Reader grabs my hand. I wasn't exactly certain why he did that until I heard one of the kids whistling and hollering.

"Reed buddy! What's up? What's new? That your girlfriend?" one of them shouts.

Reader turns to look at me.

"Please just ignore them, they aren't worth the time. Trust me."

We headed in the opposite direction to the little diner on the corner but before we got to the door, I couldn't help hearing one of them call out.

"Hey book nerd, what'd you do, knock a girl up?"

Reader squeezed my hand harder. I'm not sure if he meant for me to notice but I could tell he was getting upset. He led me to a little corner table, and we waited for our server.

"Who were those kids back there?" I asked hoping he would tell me.

"That's Chad and his goons. Chad doesn't like me because I dated his ex-girlfriend for a while after she broke up with him. He's kind of a dick. In the end she wasn't worth the energy, so we broke up. He obviously refuses to grow up."

"Oh, I see. High School drama. Fun stuff." I said, rolling my eyes.

Reader laughs.

"Yes exactly!" Rolling his eyes too.

"Please don't let him or anyone else bother you though. From what I've learned from my very short time on earth is that life is too short. That saying never proves wrong."

"Okay, I will do my best. Thanks."

"Of course."

Lunch was delicious. I ate every crumb of my burger and fries. I think it's because I'm pregnant or it could just have been the quality of the food was better here, but I've never wanted to eat so much in my life, and I've never really noticed how good food tastes until I was eating for two. Plus, I haven't had the opportunity to eat out, like at all.

We made some more small talk, but it was still a little awkward. I think Reader could sense that I didn't want to talk too much about my situation. And he doesn't press. But he also doesn't give too much of himself away either. He told me he was mostly shy growing up. His parents were both writers and he was an only child, so he spent most of his time with them, especially when they were both writing for days upon days. He had a great childhood. It was just a very quiet one. I could understand, although my dad was a very loud, mean, and intimidating man, I too spent most of my time alone. Which I didn't love. He also told me how his parents died. Which was really sad.

On the way back to the Bed and Breakfast I couldn't stop yawning. Food in my belly and this baby in my tummy made me tired all the time.

Reader put the truck into park, then helped me get out.

"Why don't you go on up and get yourself rested. Dinner isn't until six o'clock so you can take your time. I am going to catch up on yard work Lily has been after me about."

I really could use a nap.

"Thank you, Reader, really I had a great time today."

"Anytime. This was fun."

He walked in the opposite direction to the garage, and I walked through the front door, up the grand staircase and up to my room. I couldn't wait for my nap.

10

Reader

It took everything in me not to run over and punch Chad in the throat. If I had, he would have deserved it. Not just for this specific reason today but for many other reasons too. We always got along fine until Jessica came into the picture. She had just broken up with him a month before and I had never had a girlfriend before. So, I spent eight months dealing with his jealous ego bullshit before I realized she was just as toxic as he was. I dumped her and then my parents died. I've kept to myself for the last year, but Chad apparently hasn't had enough time to grow the fuck up.

I don't even care if he thinks I knocked Emily up. Hell, I'll even say I did just to protect her. I have a feeling that's what it would take for her not to get harassed. But if he even tries, he won't get a second chance.

Taking Emily to the library just made my very new feelings for her more intense. Seeing the amazement on her face really hit me in the heart strings. I love that I am the one who gets to show her all these things she's never seen before. I could get addicted to this feeling. It's a feeling I haven't felt before. The fact that she picked that poetry book off my bookshelf earlier just confirms that we might have very similar tastes in reading. I couldn't love that more. So, I loaded her up with most of my favorites at the library. I want to see how she takes to them. If she doesn't that's just fine, but my mother groomed me to love love, why couldn't I show Emily something about what real love is about too?

I spent the rest of the afternoon working in the back yard. I was happy to hear that Emily loves the Sycamore trees. Up until about a year ago, the trees were my and my mother's favorite place to sit and read. We'd bring out a blanket to lay on or sometimes folding chairs and just read for hours under the heated shade, the stream rushing in the background. I loved laying under them, looking up at them like they were skyscrapers and dreaming as I gazed at their giant green leaves that will turn yellow, orange, and then brown in the fall.

It didn't really need it, but I spent an hour making sure my favorite spot under the trees was perfectly groomed. I want her to find safety under those trees. I have a feeling she needs it.

When I was done with my chores, I headed back into the kitchen for something cold to drink. Lily was getting dinner ready.

"Hey Lily."

"Reed. How are you doing today? How's Emily."

"Great. We stopped at the library and then we grabbed lunch. She's up napping now."

"Um hmm. And has she mentioned anything to you about the child dear?"

I know she is just as curious as I am.

"No, she doesn't say a lot and I'm trying not to pry. I like her… I hope she sticks around."

Lily turns away from her stove to look at me.

"Just be careful Reed. Don't go getting' your heart broken when she takes that baby and leaves. We don't know her story. She could be fixin' to leave soon."

She turns to stir the soup.

"We won't know until she's up and gone." she whispers.

I don't know if I was meant to hear that or not, but I did, and it felt really sad.

I backed away from the kitchen slowly. I wasn't sure what I was supposed to say next. I find sometimes it's best to leave Lily with her thoughts. She struggles sometimes with missing her daughter and granddaughter. It's the worst kind of pain not knowing where they are and then one day you find out they are both dead when they showed up in two urns with a letter saying they were in a tragic accident and had died. Even many years later I know that kind of pain never dulls. I lost my parents and that's hard, I saw my parents lose a child. I lost a brother. We are no strangers to that kind of pain. I can imagine what losing a child feels like.

I just know from being around so much love and loss that if you can save someone from being alone, you save them.

11

Emily

I woke to what I thought was a soft knock on my door. I climbed or rather rolled out of bed and opened the door to find Reader standing there.

"Hey." he smiles.

"Thought maybe you'd like to know that dinner is ready."

"Oh, yeah. Thanks!"

I had almost slept through dinner.

He gives me a shrug.

"No problem."

Then he heads for the stairs.

I call after him.

"I'll be down in a few. I hope that's okay?"

He lifts an arm in the air signaling he heard me then yells, "take your time."

I bolted to the bathroom to see what I looked like in the mirror, hoping I wasn't a mess. I wasn't this time. Thank God! I used the bathroom, washed up and headed down to the kitchen for my first official dinner here at The Four-Leaf Clover Bed and Breakfast.

Lily had the table set for the three of us. I've never seen a table set for dinner. Not with the proper place settings. Fork to the left, knife, and spoon to the right… cloth napkins, pretty china, and glass cups. It felt so formal, and I loved it. For the first time ever, I felt like some sort of a family even if it wasn't true.

"I can see why this soup is a favorite Lily. It's delicious. So creamy and the dumplings are a delicious surprise. I've never had this before."

I complemented Lily's cooking, making sure I sound grateful because I was grateful.

"Thank you my dear."

I looked up at Reader who was seated across from me. He was already looking up at me. He winked. I smiled and then I felt my face heat. He smiled and looked down at his soup, taking another bite. For the first time in my life, I knew what butterflies in your stomach meant and this time it wasn't the baby kicking.

Dinner was pleasant, small talk. Lily told me more about the house and the trees. Their trees were the oldest and largest in the town. She told me about how they used to attract sightseers back in the day, but folks were finding better things to see besides trees these days. Which isn't great for the Bed and Breakfast, but she was happy she didn't need the guests to stay financially afloat.

After dinner I headed to the back gardens to start reading one of the books that Reader picked out for me at the library. I found a chair set up under the trees with a blanket set to the side, a book light, and a bottle of water. I smiled, knowing Reader did that for me. I got lost in that book for over three hours.

It was almost ten when I closed it and headed back inside. Reader was already sitting at the kitchen counter with a laptop open in front of him.

"Hey," was all he said when I walked into the house.

"Hi."

He takes a few seconds to finish up what he was typing. Then he looks back up at me.

"You look like you were enjoying that one." he said pointing at the poetry book I had in my hand.

"I was." I said slightly embarrassed but only because he still made me slightly uncomfortable to be around him.

"Let me know when you are ready to return the books we loaned out and I can take you back to get more. It's not a problem." he smiles.

"That's kind of you. Thank you."

I take a minute to think about my next words... almost chickening out.

"I was thinking... that I'd like to take out some books on raising a special needs baby."

He's still looking at me but now with alarm in his eyes. I don't think he meant to, but I know I just laid a very heavy piece of information in his lap.

"Oh... okay... yeah. Do you want to go back tomorrow for that? We can go back tomorrow if its urgent."

I appreciate his concern.

"It's not urgent but I do need to get prepared. I've got some time though." I whisper that last part.

I know I've got his full attention now and I can see he's got a list of questions on his face. Could I trust him with more details? I think I can...

"I found out at my last doctor's appointment that he has Down Syndrome."

He blinks harder. Probably not meaning to, and then I catch the shift of his Adam's apple, like this news affects him personally. Which I can imagine it does. Anyone who is a good human and hears a baby will be born with any sort of special needs would be affected. It's not news anyone is prepared for. It's just well… it's saddening. He doesn't say anything else.

"Would you maybe mind keeping this to yourself for right now? I just don't want the baby judged right off the bat before I have a chance to prepare myself."

This breaks him out of his silence.

"Yes Emily, I can. Absolutely. I will keep it to myself."

He covers his heart with his hand.

"Thank you."

He's silent for a few minutes.

"Should we try to find you a doctor… here?" he asks.

"Oh, umm… I can look into it and let you know. Thanks Reader."

"Of course."

I don't know if I can trust a new doctor. I don't know if I can trust technology these days. Everything is linked. I'll be hard enough hiding when I go into labor. If I see a doctor, the baby's real parents could possibly find me. I have a feeling they are searching for me as we speak.

"I think I'm going to head up and get some rest now."

"Alright, sounds good Emily. Library opens at ten. We can head over around then?"

I think about it for a second. Going sooner than later would probably be best and it sounds like Reader may be more anxious about it than I am. I don't want to make him worry.

"Yes, that sounds good. Thank you."

Chance Worth Taking

Our conversations still feel so formal. I trust him with my secret, not all of it but at least that part of it. But I'm still feeling intimidated around him. The chemistry is confusing. It's scary carrying around a huge secret like this. I'm terrified this baby will get taken away from me and who will love him like I will? Nobody. Nobody else will. I just can't risk that.

I also can't afford a doctor on my own. I don't have that kind of money to spend when I need to pay for housing. And after the baby is born, I will have a hospital bill to pay for. We had good care before now, Tate made sure I had the best prenatal care. They were close friends with the Doctor who monitored all my prenatal visits. So close that they were all willing to end this pregnancy once they found out he was a special needs baby. I am a bit surprised they missed it and we got this far along. I'm not too worried that this baby will need any medical attention before he decides to bless us with his presence. We only have two months left and so far, this has been an uneventful pregnancy. I just need to deliver him and hope this all works out in the best interest for both of us. I hope they all just leave us alone.

Once I climbed into bed, I could barely keep my eyes open. I gave this baby and myself what we needed and that is me well rested and then tomorrow morning we are off to the library again to start preparing.

12

Emily

We pulled into the library parking lot at exactly ten. I could tell Reader was more anxious about this than I was. I don't know if telling him was the right choice. I don't know if trusting anyone was the right choice. I know I can't hide the outcome of this baby from everybody. As soon as he is born, his Down Syndrome will be noticeable, but I could have given myself two more months to not have to bring anyone else into it. I could have waited. I might not even be here in two months. Then what have I done? I've worried Reader for no reason. I'm hoping now that I don't regret this.

Reader led me once again through the library to the baby section this time. I was impressed that he knew exactly where it was. There were four huge sections of baby books. I wanted to look through them all, not just the special needs ones. I picked out *What to expect when you are expecting* first. I had a copy at home that Tate had given me. But I had left it at home. I also grabbed *What to expect the first year*. Since I was not the baby's mother, I didn't feel like I needed to read that one before. I want to read it now. Reader handed me a small stack of books on Down Syndrome, and I grabbed a baby name book.

"You don't know yet what you want to name him?" Reader asked me as we were using the self-checkout this time.

"I guess I hadn't thought about it yet."

Marianne wasn't at her desk, so we took that opportunity to check these books out in secret. Reader also told me he could drop them back off after hours in the return drop box so nobody would ask us any questions. Maybe he was trustworthy after all.

Back in the truck, I open up the baby name book and start looking through it.

"I bet naming the baby is the best part. Unless you couldn't decide then I am sure that is probably stressful."

"Well wish me luck!" I laugh.

"Good luck! At least you've narrowed it down to a boy."

"Yes, that makes it a lot easier for sure." I agreed.

When we returned to the house, I took off to the gardens to start reading. Reader needed to help Lily with some things so he said he would meet me later to read poetry and to give my brain a break from the information overload I was about to experience.

He was of course right. There was so much to take in. Raising a baby, especially one with special needs, was going to be hard. Harder because I am on my own. I don't know how I will even begin to do this alone. I don't think I had even realized when I took this baby and ran, what I was getting myself into. And I could never understand how they could terminate a baby they so desperately wanted, especially one this far along. I am not against free choice, but if we are talking about me, my body and this baby, my choice is pro this baby. Besides, if the baby was born now, he'd most likely survive. I can't consciously do that to him. I'd never forgive myself. What they were asking me to do now just felt wrong. They were asking me to deliver the baby, a baby they were purposely going to end his life.

It was hard enough that I was okay with being the surrogate to start with. It wasn't really even my choice. My father manipulated me into it. He told me I would get the money. He told me this would be my way out. He told me this was how I would be able to make my life better. Better than it would be if I stayed in the town we were in. He sold me on this bigger and better dream. He sold me on escaping. He also knew it was only a matter of time before I left home. I had been saving every dollar that I could to leave. He knew I worked crummy jobs when I could just to try and leave one day. So, he lied to me. He painted me this beautiful picture. He painted me a forty thousand dollar get away plan. Painted me this picture that he cared. That Tate and Alicia cared. He applied the pressure. But once I was implanted with the baby and it was a viable pregnancy, he took the money for himself. He had never planned on giving it to me and Tate and Alicia... they could care less who they were paying. They just needed an heir for their family's wealth so that it didn't go to somebody in the family that they didn't like. Alicia had apparently miscarried too many times. So, my father, who works landscaping for them at their small-town mansion in rural West Virginia, offered them a solution they couldn't refuse. They compared costs, decided my father's offer was a good deal and they paid off a doctor to perform the implanting of the fertilized egg and to oversee the pregnancy. Nobody will know that when the baby was born that Alicia wasn't the one carrying him or the one who didn't deliver him. They had the perfect plan to pull this whole scheme off. My father only scheming for the money at my expense.

But things took a turn when they started to get nervous about the baby's size and how little he moved. So, they did a bunch of tests and it came back not in their favor. It turned out to be their worst nightmare. Especially Alicia's.

The pregnancy was to be terminated the following weekend after doctors' hours. I would still receive the money that was owed to me after the delivery.

But I left.

Now I... my father... will not be getting the money.

Because I ran. I ran *with* the baby.

They are filthy rich but what they did was illegal in so many ways. I am sure they could win any case they presented against me, paying off everyone if they needed to, but then they would take the chance of people finding out about what they did. I don't think that humility is something that they would want to live with. Not for their prestigious social life that would be worse than raising a son with Down Syndrome.

Reader met me under the trees shortly after one. He brought sandwiches, two smaller bags of chips and two cans of orange soda. He also brought a book with him. Not one that we checked out at the library.

"So, are you keeping a secret stash of books from me?" I teased recognizing the book in his hand from two nights ago.

He smiles.

He picks it back up from where he set it down a few minutes ago.

"I thought maybe since you trusted me with a secret, I would trust you with one of mine."

"Oh, okay."

Lorinda Faye

I was curious.

"This is a book of poems I've written, they are all very personal but, I thought if you'd like I could read you one?"

He's asking?

Wow!

I am equally shocked and excited.

"Yes, yes please! I would love that."

"Okay great, here goes..."

Reader clears his throat and then begins reading...

There were supposed to be four names etched in these walls,
Carved into wood, in whispered halls,
Tucked into old books and birthdays too,
Now only mine echoes in the rooms we once knew.

The wind still knocks and calls for you,
On the porch like it always used to,
It still whips through the tall trees,
But no one answers it but me.

I am the one left over and torn,
The frayed end of a story unborn,
A cradle sat quiet and bare,
The silence too heavy, thick with prayer.

Sometimes I talk to the stars above,
Like they're listening, in love,
Not cold pinholes in the sky turned black,
But keepers of the ones we cannot get back.

I wonder if ghosts ever tire so,
Waiting for us to finally let go,

Chance Worth Taking

I wonder what it means to belong, to stay,
In a world that keeps moving forward anyway.

Still, I breathe,
I write,
I remember,
I still.

And maybe that's enough for now,
Or maybe it's just what the living will allow,
To carry the weight, afraid to sever,
Holding on to goodbye forever.

I sat there is complete awe the whole time that he was reading to me. He is an exceptionally talented writer. I don't have any experience to say I know how to judge a good writer from a bad one, but he had me wrapped into him the whole time he was reading.

I was in shock.

"Wow Reader, I don't know where to begin."

He smiles at me. He's got his eyes locked on mine.

"Well, I just wanted to share something I wrote with you. This last year hasn't been easy on me, and I guess I just wanted you to know that I can probably relate if you ever needed or wanted to talk."

His words are genuine; I can tell that for sure. I've spent enough time with a man whose words were nothing close to genuine, so I know that Reader's are in fact, genuine.

"I appreciate that." I whispered because I'm afraid if I speak up that my voice will shake.

He takes my response to change the subject.

"Will you do me a favor?"

His question catches me off guard and confuses me. I don't know what favor I could do for him. But I want to.

"Sure."

"Can I read those books after you, before I return them? I'd like to know what you are in for... you know just in case you are still here when he's born. Will you still be here when he is born?"

I didn't know the answer to that question.

All I could say was, "Oh... I hope so."

"I hope so too."

Then he stands up, picks up the sandwich plates and his drink and walks back up to the house leaving me sitting under the Sycamore trees alone.

He wants me to stay?

13

Reader

R eading those baby books made me sad. Not in the way that you think. More in a saddening way of missing someone you never had an opportunity to see grow up.

For whatever reason Emily chose to keep this baby boy. I am not sure if she had ever entertained the idea of not keeping him, but I am so glad she didn't choose not to.

I can't help but feel like I am meant to have some part in this baby's life. I have been going to therapy for the last seven months to help with losing my parents. My therapist tells me that I am feeling this way about Emily and her baby to fill the void of my family not being here. It's not right or wrong to feel this way, but it's definitely a strong enough feeling that I need to seek out the true meaning and find my true intentions.

We decided that I would tell Emily about my baby brother, just to get it off my chest. I just needed to find the right time. Since his birthday was coming up in a few days, I decided I'll do it then.

***

Emily was lying under the Sycamore trees reading when I approached her. She looked up at me with a smile, one I've already gotten very used to.

"Hey Reader."

"Hey Em. How are you liking the book?"

The day before I had given her my mother's first novel to read. I was hoping she would love it like I do.

"Reader this is amazing! I can't put it down! How Ember waits for her true love to come back to her... but then gets trapped with this Adam guy... oh my gosh! I'm dying to find out how it ends!"

I loved that she loved it so far.

"She wrote that book before I was born but it's message stands the test of love time."

"Love time?" I asked confused.

"Yeah, like over time when love is true, time cannot change it. It's just something kind of silly my mother used to say."

I was really hoping she understood what I meant.

"Oh yeah, that is true. I get it."

"Good." I said as I laid on my side facing her. She was already in her usual side lying position. I usually lay flat on my back. This time I wanted to see her.

She must have understood the intention because she closed the book and looked at me with concern.

She smiled searching my face.

"Reader is everything okay?"

"Yeah, just a hard day which is actually why I came out here."

"Okay. What is it?"

"Um, so today is kind of an important day for my family... well was for my family. It still is for me since I am obviously the only one here." I rambled.

I said that trying to keep things light, but I think she took it heavy because she reached out and grabbed my hand. A feeling I really liked.

"Is today the day your parents passed?" she asked.

"No... no, not my parents."

"Okay..."

I took a deep breath; Emily is the first person I have talked about this with besides my therapist.

"When I was thirteen my mom got pregnant with my baby brother. We were all really excited. We had everything ready for him, and she had an easy pregnancy, no issues. She went into labor just fine. But when he was born, something must have happened because he was still born. Today is his birthday. He would have been six if he would have made it."

"Oh Reader! I am so sorry. That is... heartbreaking! Truly. I can't even imagine how that had felt or how that feels now."

"It doesn't feel good. Especially since both my parents are gone now too. It would have been nice to at least have a little brother around."

"I'm so sorry." Emily whispers.

Her words release a tear from my eye, and it makes its way down my left cheek. I just stared at her, ignoring the tear. She makes me feel safe in my vulnerability, which is new for me.

"What was his name?"

I take a deep breath. I haven't said his name out loud in so long.

"Marshall."

Emily smiles and it relaxes me.

She releases my hand and wipes the tear with the back of her hand.

"He's kicking me pretty hard right now. Do you want to feel?"

My breath catches so hard I stop breathing. I really do want to feel him kick.

I get the words out finally.

"I do."

Emily grabs my hand again and sets it down on her very round stomach. Sure enough, he met my hand with a few strong kicks.

I laugh and this makes Emily laugh too.

We both feel his kicks for a while before it gets serious again.

"I'm so sorry you lost your little brother Reader, and your parents. I lost my mom when I was four. So, I can also relate. I don't have any siblings, but I suppose that is a good thing since my father is not a good guy. I always thought it was better that it was only me so nobody else got hurt."

I like her opening up to me.

"I'm so sorry Emily."

"Thanks. So do you do anything special for his birthday?"

"I do. It's what I'm doing right now. My mother and I used to sit under the trees, and I would read poems."

"Did you bring them?"

"I did."

"Do you want to read one to me?"

Reader sits up and reaches behind him for his journal.

"Sure."

Chance Worth Taking

You never took a breath in time,
But you still take away mine,
Every year when the page of a calendar turns,
I wonder who you would have been.

Would you have my eyes,
Our fathers laugh,
Would you love like momma,
Chase fireflies with fists full of wonder.

You came in silence,
But not emptiness,
Your name unspoken in most circles,
But never erased in mine.

You are inked in memory,
And stitched into the quiet corners,
I see you in the stream,
And you are spoken into the roots.

Every year that passes,
I imagine frosting on your cheeks,
A candle flickering,
And me beside you.

Not as a boy who lost everything,
But as your big brother,
Your perfect soul mate,
Who got to love you anyway.

You didn't stay,
But you are still here,

Lorinda Faye

In the way I pause at sunsets,
In a way I'll never forget,

So Happy birthday, little one,
Today is your day, I'll carry your wish for you,
And promise to live in all the ways
you never got the chance to do.

When I got done reading, Emily was the one in tears.

"I'm sorry I didn't mean to upset you."

Emily lays back again and so do I.

"I'm so sorry about your brother."

"Thanks."

Emily takes a deep breath. I know she's got something on her mind. I can feel it.

"Tell me what you are thinking." I asked quietly hoping she would open up.

"I'm just thinking about how my life could have gone for me and this baby verse the way it went. I feel like I've spent most of my life so far, trying to escape where I came from. And then I found you and Lily, and it's changed me so much. I believe that happiness is possible for the first time in my life. It's just... I don't know. I thought it wasn't going to get better, ever. I didn't think it could, not after this. I'm so happy I'm here."

I know she meant the baby when she said *this*. I wanted to know more. I felt like maybe it was the right time.

"Does he have a father?"

There was silence that felt like it lasted forever before she answered.

"No Reader, there's no father. It's just us."

It's just us.

I know she meant just her and the baby. But I wanted it to mean just the three of us. I wanted it to mean that really badly.

We lay there that afternoon until we both fell asleep. Hope in my heart for the first time in a long time.

- 65 -

14

Emily

The next morning I woke up to Reader knocking on my door.

"Yeah." I called out.

He popped his head in.

"Hey get up. It's beach day." he said with a huge smile.

Wait what?

"Really? Wait, you're going to take me to the beach for my first time in my life when I'll look like a beached whale?"

I was obviously teasing. I really wanted to go.

He walked towards my bed as I started to sit up. I was awake but had been laying there for about an hour reading.

"Well lucky for us beached whales are in this year." he teases back.

I scoff.

"So, you do think I look like a whale! That's nice to know."

Then I threw my book at him.

Luckily, he caught it. I got so caught up in the flirty moment otherwise I would have never thrown a book.

"Wow."

Reader's face turns to shock.

"That's book abuse you know. You could have your library card revoked. I think I'll tell Marianne on you."

"You wouldn't!" I fired back.

"I would!"

"I'd never forgive you!"

"Well, I'd never forgive you if you don't get up and get ready right now. Everything is packed, so come on, let's go!"

I pull the covers off and stand up.
"Bossy, aren't you?"

He laughs.

"Maybe, but today is all about you. We're going to do everything that can be done on the beach, starting with swimming in the ocean, sun tanning, and then building a sandcastle."

Standing up reminds me that I feel like I'm a thousand pounds.

"You did notice that I am actually the size of an actual whale. I can't even bend over anymore."

"I noticed."

He winks then adds...

"If you want you can just watch me do all the things. I'll even let you take all the credit."

"Now that sounds like a good deal. Can I have like twenty minutes?"

"Yup. Meet me downstairs. I've packed breakfast. We can eat in the car."

"Okay."

Omg! The beach!

I don't think I've been this excited about anything in my whole life. The only experience I have with the beach is what my momma told me when I was four. It was her experience. If she told me anything different about it before then, I wouldn't remember.

I know it was her favorite place to go. She told me she would go every weekend growing up when school was out. Summers were her favorite time, and she lived in her pretty swimsuits.

That memory flashed through my mind as I was looking for something to wear. I didn't own a swimsuit this size and the one I do have; it is back in West Virginia. It wouldn't fit me anyways.

I was immediately flooded with sadness. My first time at a beach and I had to go in a giant t-shirt and elastic shorts.

Swallowing my pity down, I got dressed, fixed my hair into a ponytail and grabbed my shoes.

Reader was standing in the front entry when I finally made it downstairs.

"Ready?"

"Ready as I'll ever be."

I pushed out in a sigh.

Reader gave me a funny look then turned towards the door.

"Come on. We have a lot to do today."

I guess I was still a bit sour about the circumstances. This was not how I imagined this moment. But I never imagined it with Reader either. So maybe the disappointment evens out?

Reader had packed breakfast wraps.

"Did you make these?" I asked, examining mine after I took a bite. There was sausage, eggs, cheese, and spinach all rolled up in a wrap. It was delicious.

"I sure did! Slaved all morning over them too!"

I saw the corner of his mouth lift then I heard him chuckle. The one I am getting pleasantly familiar with.

"Liar."

"Okay fine, Lily made them. But only because she wanted to help."

I looked over at him in shock.

"You were totally going to take all the credit, weren't you?"

He turns and winks at me and my stomach flutters. I know it's not the baby because the baby kicks hard these days. These are actual butterflies.

"Maybe."

I feel my face redden and then I find it hard to eat. But I take a bite anyway so he doesn't see me flustered.

The drive was a good two hours long. We took turns picking songs. He picked his favorites and then I picked mine. Sometimes we would sing and sometimes he would just sing. And I found myself falling for him quickly. It felt exciting.

For my whole life all I wanted was to go to the beach. I wanted to remember my momma's stories and I wanted to feel her presence. I didn't feel her anywhere. Not in my home back in West Virginia, not through my father, not now with her locket around my neck in a town she had probably been in at some point in her life.

I believed deeply that I'd feel her at the beach. I was beyond excited now that this day had finally come no matter the circumstances.

We pulled into this small town called Isle of Palms. Reader entered the beach parking lot and found a spot to park. The parking lot wasn't full so maybe the beach wouldn't be so busy. I don't know why I'm worried. I feel embarrassed maybe. Guilty? Ashamed? I've closed myself off to anyone but Reader and Lily. Not that I had a lot of people who cared about me anyway, the thought of being around people who might judge me felt scary.

Once we exit the car Reader locks it. I heard the car beep.

"Don't we need our stuff?" I questioned.

He walks over to me and grabs my hand. A gesture I can get used too.

"We do but first were going to grab you a swimsuit at the beach store."

Shocked and then embarrassed, I asked quietly, "Do you think they will have one that fits me?"

Reader smiles and starts to pull me towards the parking lot exit.

"I do. I've already called ahead and asked. They have a couple of maternity suits for you to choose from."

I instantly stopped walking causing Reader to pull on my arm.

"You did that?"

I'm shocked.

He turns towards me and sets both of his hands on my upper arms. Then he looks me in the eyes.

"I did because you deserve to have the absolute best first beach day experience and you don't need to be going in this over-sized shirt. Besides how will you fry like a lobster if you wear that?"

I laugh.

"What? Are you serious? People fry themselves here?"

"Pretty much any girl who comes to the beach for the first day that I've known, fry's herself on the first day. It happens every time. I figured you'd want the same experience?" he winks.

I shake my head no.

"I think that's one beach tradition I'd like to skip if I could?"

Reader grabs my hand again and we walk together toward the strip of stores. We pass by people who smile at us. To them we probably look like a young couple in love, having a baby. What I feared at first about being judged, I think I was wrong. Reader makes me feel safe. He makes everything okay.

The beach store was big and bright. Racks and racks of clothes. Beach themed items, sandals, chairs, trinkets, anything you could possibly think of was probably in this store.

"Okay so on the list..."

Wait, there's a list?

"...swimsuit, swim cover, sandals, beach towels, sunscreen, sunglasses, two beach chairs, an umbrella, and a souvenir. Let's do this!"

I paused stunned.

"Wait, Reader I didn't bring that much money with me. I'm sorry, I didn't know we were doing all of this."

He pulls me deeper into the store.

"I know. And it's on me. This is my day to give to you. That means all the bells and whistles too. We can't beach without any of it."

We stop at the swimsuits rack first that has a big sign on it that says maternity. He starts separating the clothing on the rack looking them over.

"Are you sure?" I asked worried that I was an inconvenience. I've never had anyone like this spend money on me.

This felt weird to me. Accepting kindness when I've never really experienced kindness before felt weird and unnatural.

He's still shuffling through the suits.

"Yep, I'm sure."

He pulls a plum-colored suit off the rack and holds it up. It's pretty. It has an opening right under where my chest is, separating the top from the bottom, giving it a bikini vibe but still a one piece.

"How about this one?"

He sees my eyes light up.

"It's pretty."

"Great! One thing done!"

Before I can say anything else he walks away. I follow him around the store while he gathers all the things. He makes me try on a couple different pairs of sunglasses and sandals, to see which ones I liked best, but he is not giving me any room to object. I made the mistake of picking up a seashell ankle bracelet. He took it out of my hands so fast that I didn't have any time to react. All he said was *shhh... we're getting it* before heading to the registers.

He pays for the items, then asks the cashier where the changing room was. She pointed to the back left corner of the store. He hands me the suit and swimsuit cover and walks over to the changing rooms with me.

He smiles wide. It feels like he is more excited than I am about this. Truth is I am a bit worried. I think I had envisioned this all to be perfect, but with the way things are for me now, I was afraid. Afraid to be disappointed. Afraid to be let down. Not by anyone or anything. Just by my own expectations of my first experience here.

Once inside the changing room, I slowly undressed. This was the biggest mirror I had ever been in front of. I was taken back by the sight of me. My stomach was firm and large. My breasts were full. My hips, bigger than they ever have been. I don't think I've gained too much weight. Last time I checked at the doctor's office, I had only gained twenty-two pounds. Maybe I am around thirty now. Regardless, I actually don't think I look as bad as I thought I did. I think most of my thoughts were just my insecurities creeping in and wreaking havoc on myself.

I pulled the suit over my legs and up my body. Once my arms were in, I fixed the part my chest goes in, straightening everything out. Then I just stood there and stared at my reflection.

"Everything okay in there?"

Reader probably realized I was a little too quiet.

I stared more. A tear runs down my cheek.

"Yes Reader. It's perfect!"

15

Emily

I exit the dressing room with my new suit and the cover up on. Reader took the tags off my sandals and my sunglasses. He held the now empty bag open for me to put my other clothes and shoes in. I've never seen him smile this much.

"So, are you ready for this?"

I'm ready for everything if it's with you.

"I am."

"Alright let's go to the beach!"

Before we made it back to the car, we detoured for ice cream cones. Reader said we had to. There's nothing that screams summer and beach louder than an ice cream cone. I think I agree with him. I've only had two in my entire life. This is my third. I didn't tell him that. He had such a happy childhood. I didn't want to ruin his good mood by telling him my dad wasn't a *take his daughter for ice cream* kind of dad. That would spark more questions and ultimately lead to him knowing my father was more abusive and manipulating than I said earlier. I wasn't ready for him to know that much about me. Plus, this day was supposed to be fun and light. I wanted to keep it that way.

"You have a little chocolate on your chin."

"I do?"

Embarrassed, I wiped my face hoping it was gone.

"Did I get it?"

Reader looks then smiles.

"Nope. Here let me help you."

Reader brings his napkin up to my face and wipes the ice cream off my chin. This kind of closeness makes me nervous.

"Thank you." I whisper, hoping he can't hear my heart pumping faster. It's all I can hear. It sounds like it's going to pump out of my chest.

Reader smiles and that's the last thing I saw before his lips were on mine. I closed my eyes and just let him kiss me. When he finally pulled away, I couldn't breathe. My chest was rising and falling as fast as my heart was beating. He chuckles.

"That good huh?"

I open my eyes.

"Uh... yeah..."

It was all I could say.

He laughs then grabs my hand again as we walked the rest of the way to the car to grab the rest of our stuff.

The beach was busy but not overly crowded. Reader took off his shoes to walk in the sand.

"Geeze, the sand is hot."

He grimaces as he walks faster to find a spot to put our things down. I catch up and set down what I was carrying. Then I take a moment to take in the ocean.

The sound alone gives me chills but in a good way. Reader sees me shiver.

"Are you cold?"

I barely hear him.

"Earth to Emily? I can go back and get you a sweat-shirt?"

Before he gets too carried away, I answer him back.

"No, I'm not cold. I'm perfect. Thank you."

Satisfied, he sets up my chair. Then his. Then he sets up the umbrella. Digging a hole in the sand to anchor it.

"Don't want you to get too hot or worse burnt." he winks.

Everything he is doing looks a bit extreme, but the fuss also feels kind of nice. Nobody's fussed over me before.

I sit down in my chair and take off my sandals, setting my feet on top of the sand. I dig my toes in and out, getting a real feel of the phrase *sand in my toes.* It was everything I expected and more. The warmth was a different kind of warm. It was a happy warm. Comfortable. Like I was supposed to be there. I don't know how this day could get any better.

Reader is still busy setting up our little beach space up.

"Does everyone go to all this trouble?"

Reader opens the cooler and pulls out a flavored water and hands it to me.

"Stay hydrated please."

I laugh.

"So that's a no?"

I look around and finally take in the crowd. Everyone here is relaxed, laughing, wet, playing, running, yelling, everything fun you could think of doing at a beach is being done. Then I take in their beach sets ups...

"I guess that is a yes." I answer myself.

"Yes, it's great, isn't it?"

"It really is."

I twist off the cap to my water and take a sip, and then another.

"Are you hungry?"

"Nope, I'm good thanks. The ice cream filled me up for now."

"Do you want me to put the cooler under your feet to put your feet up?"

"No thanks. I'm okay for now."

"How about a book to read, I brought you a couple books."

"Not right now, thanks."

"How about..."

"Can we go in the ocean?" I asked interrupting him.

"Yes! Absolutely!"

He starts to take off his shirt. This is the first time I've seen his bare chest. He's lean and muscular, and the sight of him makes my stomach flip. I'm attracted, for sure affected. I stood up and followed his lead taking off my swimsuit cover. I feel so much more confident than I have in a long time. *He's* made me feel more confident than I have in a long time.

Once our extra clothes were off, he reaches out for my hand and together we walk towards the ocean.

We reach the water's edge, and I feel it pool between my toes. I look down and instantly get dizzy.

"Whoa! What is happening?"

Reader laughs.

"It's a weird feeling, isn't it? Feels like you are moving but you aren't, the ocean is."

"It's so weird!"

"Just look up."

"Okay."

He pulls my arm gently.

"Come on let's get in. Just watch for jellyfish. They will sting you."

I pull back.

"Wait seriously?"

"Yeah, have you never heard of jellyfish?"

"Well yes I have, but I thought they were like out there." I say as I point to the middle of the ocean.

"You know, with the sharks."

Reader smiles.

"Oh yeah, I forgot, watch out for the sharks too!"

"What? No! I'm not going in there then."

I started to back up. Reader resists by pulling my arm and body back to him, pulling me in close.

"Emily, it's mostly a joke. Sometimes a shark will come close to the shore but it's rare. Plus, we will see it first and the jellyfish are harder to see but we will be okay. It's not worth not swimming in the ocean over."

"I don't know." I hesitate, still not convinced.

"I'm scared now. I thought the ocean was safe."

"It is safe. We will be okay; we don't have to go that far out. Let's just go up to our waists for right now."

"Are you sure we will be okay?"

"Yes, I am sure. And if we do get stung hopefully it's me and not you."

My eyes widen.

"That doesn't help."

He laughs and pulls me towards the ocean waves. I sigh and follow behind trusting him completely.

The water is waist deep, but the waves crash hard. Every time one comes in and hits me, I stretch myself taller.

"Just let it hit you."

I try...

"It's cold."

"It feels good."

A wave comes in and hits Reader in the face.

I let the next one do the same. Then I spit.

"Yuck! That's not good. Ewe. Do you like that?"

I spit more trying to get the oceans taste out of my mouth.

"I don't mind. It's just salt."

"Salt and jellyfish poop." I joke.

Reader splashes me in the face, soaking me.

"Hey! Not nice!"

He laughs.

"I'm just giving you the full beach experience. You said this is what you wanted."

"I did. But with maybe less jellyfish poop and to not be shark bait. It would eat me first because I am two people, while you're just one."

Reader thinks about that.

"Good point. Ready to get out?"

"One hundred percent."

We spent the next six hours soaking up the sun, walking the beach, and collecting seashells. He made me play frisbee because that was part of the beach experience. We snacked a lot. He also read me poetry while I closed my eyes and let the sun kiss my face. I admittedly fell asleep, twice. Then we built a sandcastle together. It was a pretty big one. It had four towers. One on each corner and it had a moat, where water could pass through. We even found sticks and snack wrappers to use for flags. It was a great sandcastle. When we were done, we gave it to a couple of little kids who were set up next to us. They were so excited until one of them accidentally knocked down one of the towers. After that they decided they had enough fun, so they stepped on the whole thing, flattening it like it never had once existed.

It was by far the best day of my life. Reader promised to take me back as soon as he could. When we got home, it was a quick dinner and an early bedtime for me. All that fresh air and sunshine wiped me completely out.

16

Emily

R eader and I fell into a routine. In the mornings I
would read everything I could get my hands on
since I couldn't do much else. We made a few more trips
back and forth to the library and the beach. He would
spend his mornings helping Lily with things she needed
help with, and I just read, ate until my belly was full, and
enjoyed their company. I started to look forward to it so
much that I had forgotten about the things that were
wrong in my life. I had forgotten that this baby wasn't
mine. I had forgotten about Tate and Alicia, and I had forgotten about my father. I decided a while back after he
wouldn't stop calling me, to disconnect my cell phone. I
didn't have anyone who needed to call me anyway. If I ever
needed a new one, I would just get one then. For now, my
days were full of reading, Reader, Lily, the trees, and
laughter.

He would read me poems under the trees, and when he
thought I wasn't paying attention he would change the
words to the most ridiculous words he could think of to
see if I would notice. Sometimes I would notice right away

and sometimes it would take a while. Usually when he started laughing was when I would catch on that he did it. Then things would turn into a serious conversation. Sometimes about life in general, the good and the bad. Sometimes about our dreams and ambitions. Which didn't feel like much at the time. Sometimes it would be about the baby. But most of the time we would end up lying side by side, me on my side, which was best for the baby, him on his back just talking about anything we could think up. Mostly useless questions like if we were born with different color teeth other than white, what color would we want them to be? I said teal because teal was pretty, and he said black. Because then if he ever lost a tooth, nobody would ever notice. I got way more comfortable at the beach, not worried about other people's opinions and I no longer worried about sharks and jellyfish.

That is how we spent most of our days until one day I overheard a conversation Lily was having with Reader in the kitchen. A conversation that changed how I felt about everything.

I didn't mean to eavesdrop, but they must not have heard me come down the stairs after my recurring, before dinner nap. Lily was speaking...

"Something feels off with that girl Reed. Just be cautious please. It's been a joy having her here and I certainly like the effect she's having on you. I know you need someone you can relate to and bond with. You seem happier since she's been here. Still, something feels off about her. I can't put my finger on it, but it's there."

I didn't let Lily get any further with the conversation before I turned around and quietly headed back up and then descended the stairs again, this time a bit louder. Both Lily and Reader turned to look at me.

"Oh, good dear, you are up. Dinner is about ready."

This is the first time since I've been here that I didn't feel totally welcome. I only had a couple of weeks left before this baby's due date and trying to move out now would be misery. I never thought that I would be this kind of a problem here. So far, I thought everyone was happy that I was staying here, possibly long term. As a matter of fact, it was Lily's idea for me to stay. I was thinking about leaving after three weeks and she was the one who told me to stay, that the baby and I were both welcome for as long as we needed it. She even had her church group donate baby things so that I had all the baby necessities to set up in my room for when he came. Now it felt like I should go.

I can't say anything now because then she will know that I was listening to their conversation, and I don't want them to think I can't be trusted or that they can't speak freely in their own home. But I am obviously bothered. I think Reader could tell. He is looking at me like I've grown a horn on my head.

He leans over the table and whispers to me while Lily is dishing up our dinner plates.

"Are you okay? Is the baby okay?" he asks.

"Yes, why?"

"You seem off or upset or something."

"I do?"

"Yeah, you do."

"No, I'm fine."

"Are you sure?"

I gave him a half smile. It was all I could muster up.

"I'm sure."

He leans back to his place at the table just before Lily joins us with dinner.

We eat in mostly silence, except for a little small talk.

After dinner I decided to take a walk. Getting some fresh air would do me and the baby some good. He was getting heavy though. I had already gained thirty-eight pounds. I was also getting anxious about his arrival. I'm in no way prepared for this kind of responsibility. I was just supposed to carry him to term and then my job was done. I would have still tried to take some of the birth money they gave my father, and I still would have left. I would have ran as far away as possible. I did do that; except I did it *with* the baby. Not without.

I didn't make it far when I heard Reader call after me.

"Em, hold up."

I exhaled then stopped and turned around to wait for him. When he caught up with me, I could see that he was still concerned with my distance.

"Emily, talk to me. Please?" he begs.

"What's wrong."

"Nothing. I'm fine. We're fine." I reassured him.

"You don't seem fine."

"I am."

"Okay."

Just when I think he is going to let it go...

"You'd tell me if things weren't fine, wouldn't you?"

I didn't want to lie to him. And if I was being honest, I don't know if he feels the same way as Lily does but I'm afraid to ask him. I think I'm afraid of the answer. I'm afraid of the answer because I think I am in love with him. I know I am. I just feel better about everything when I am around him. I think he does too. And Lily notices it as well.

I think I'm afraid that this will all go away once they both find out the truth, if they find out the truth. Lily's already suspicious, I can't let them find out the truth.

"I would."

He studies my face then gives me a smile, satisfied that I didn't just lie to him.

"I'm feeling extra tired tonight, I think I'm just going to go lay down for the night. Check in early. This kid has been extra active today..."

"Of course. I'll walk with you back to the house."

We both turned to walk back to the house. Reader walked beside me as usual except this time he grabbed my hand and held it until we got to the back door. Then he let it go. That's the first time I felt regret. Regret for lying to him.

***

The warm weather must have gotten people moving because the next day we had new guests arrive at the Bed and Breakfast. The first ones since the entire time that I had been here. It was a middle-aged couple who were traveling for work and decided that they wanted to stop near Charleston but preferred not to stay in the city. They would be with us for a week. They chose the Elvis room.

They were bubbly and loud and joined us every morning for breakfast and almost every evening for dinner. They talked a lot. So much that when they mistook Reader and I as a couple, none of us could get a word in to correct them. Reader and I eventually found ourselves excusing ourselves as quickly as we could and hiding out under the trees.

Our talks became mostly about the baby. Mostly about Readers' concerns. I wasn't as concerned. I couldn't be. I'd drive myself crazy.

"You don't think you should see a doctor before you go into labor?"

"I wasn't planning on it. I've seen the doctor enough to know what to expect."

"It's just the nearest hospital is an hour away. What if there is bad traffic or what if something is wrong with the baby? What if he delivers too fast?"

I laugh at his concerns. I know I shouldn't, but I wasn't expecting anyone to be more nervous than I was. He has a good reason to be though.

"It's all going to work out Reader. I know it is." I try to assure him.

I am laid back under the trees looking up towards the sky. I have spent a lot of time in this position lately. Looking up into the endless sky. This is the calmest my mind has been in my entire life.

Reader is lying next to me. He's holding my hand. Twenty minutes later I felt myself lying in a puddle of water. I'm now eating my words.

17

Emily

*M**y water just broke.*

Holy shit, my water just broke.

"Reader. Did you hear me?"

"Reader. Hello? Can you help me?

I snap my fingers, breaking Reader out of his nap.

"What's wrong?"

"My water just broke!"

"Are you joking?"

"No! Why would I joke?"

Reader jumps up springing to action.

He gives me his arm, and we walk up to the house. I change my clothes, Reader grabs my labor bag from my room, and then we head to the hospital, the contractions getting close and closer.

***

I look down at this perfect baby boy that I just delivered less than an hour ago. He's perfect to me. That's all that matters and he's mine. I know in my heart that he is. I want him, they don't, and I highly doubt they will come looking for him.

"He's just so perfect, isn't he?"

Reader's voice disrupts my thinking. I look up at him and really look at his face. I can't be upset with him anymore. I just can't. He's here right now and that is proof enough that he wants to be here. Maybe I misunderstood how he felt. Maybe I got scared and jumped to conclusions. Maybe I should have asked him about it and let him explain.

"Are you okay?" he asks quietly.

I shake my thoughts away, ready to let those doubts go.

"Yes, sorry. Yes, he is perfect. Absolutely perfect."

"I love him already."

He loves him?

His words caught me off guard. I wasn't expecting them.

"You do?" I asked to make sure I heard him right.

He shakes his head yes.

"Oh..."

The thought made me smile. This baby went from nobody wanting him to two people loving him instantly. I loved that for him.

Reader reached out and grabbed my hand.

"I can't help it, Emily"

He squeezes my hand, but I was still frozen from his words.

"Did you zone off again?" he laughs.

It stirs the baby.

He stands up, bends down, and kisses the baby on top of his head.

"You should probably get some rest. You look tired, no offense. Do you want me to take him for a bit while you sleep? I can hold him for a while."

I was exhausted. Labor and delivery took seven hours. I also knew I would get less sleep when we went home. Even though I didn't want to give him up so quickly, I let Reader take him for an hour.

When I woke up, it had been three.

Reader has never seen me naked before. It has been hard to keep any form of dignity with myself since he saw me sitting in a pool of my own amniotic fluid back at the house. He helped me change out my clothes, he was here for the delivery, and now after delivery I didn't see the point in hiding myself completely when I breastfed. I didn't feel like he was looking at me sexually anyways, not in this moment. It felt like his concern was my health and the baby's health.

When I woke up, he helped me latch the baby onto my breast like the nurse showed us. Him reading all those baby books will come in handy. Once the baby was latched on, we continued to make small talk.

"What do you think you want to name him?"

Even though I said I was unsure of his name, I felt like I needed more time. I had an idea but the name I was thinking about came with some honesty. Honesty, I haven't yet shared with Reader. I was starting to feel bad about that.

"I'm not sure yet, I think I need a little more time to see who he is first."

I looked up and smiled at Reader hoping he understood.

"Then take all the time you need."

He stood up and stretched his arms out.

"I think I'm going to go find a vending machine somewhere. Do you want anything?"

"No thanks. I'm good for now."

He bent down and kissed me on the forehead, then on the babies. Then he walked out of the room.

I stared at this beautiful baby boy lying in my arms. This feels natural. It feels right. I wonder if the plan had gone ahead like it was supposed to and Tate and Alicia had kept him, how this would feel for me? Would I feel a gaping hole in my soul? Would I miss him instantly or would my body know that he was only with me for a brief time and would I go on as usual with life?

I wonder about these things because honestly, I still don't know if what I did was the right thing to do. It feels like it was. But technically it could still be considered a crime. A crime I don't want to get caught committing.

Reader was back in fifteen minutes. That was enough time to decide that I wanted to ask him for something. Something important. Something that was a lot.

"You know you can ask me anything. Just do it. Don't hesitate, please."

"Okay, so I was wondering if it would be okay, or if you would be okay with it if I named you as the father on his birth certificate?"

I held my breath as I waited for his answer. I could see his facial expression change and I was unsure if it was a good thing. Then he smiled.

"I would be honored Emily."

"Really?"

A rush of relief washed over me.

"Really. Yes!" he sat down again.

He rubbed the baby's head with his hand.

"Nothing would make me happier."

I was happy too.

"I know what I want to name him."

"You do?"

"Yes... Chance."

"I love it. Why Chance though?"

"Because I feel like we all are getting a second chance at life and happiness."

"I love that, Em. It's perfect!"

"I want his middle name to be Marshall."

Readers' eyes filled with tears. He bent down and kissed me on the lips. With his face still so close to mine, he closed his eyes and whispered...

"I don't think I've ever been happier."

My chest tightened, the kind of ache that feels like the love I so desperately wanted finally found a home.

"I feel the same."

For the first time ever, I felt like a real family.

They let me go home the next day. Back to the Bed and Breakfast.

Reader and I settled into another routine. A different one where everything became about the baby. He stayed in his room, and I stayed in mine with Chance. He was helpful through the nights since he stayed up late anyways. He would take him downstairs with him and bring him back up to me when he went to bed. I was able to sleep most of the night, and he slept in in the mornings. During the day he still had to help Lily with her tasks. For the most part things stayed fairly normal, and I even caught Lily doting on him every once in a while. I think she finally warmed up to us.

I got so consumed with the baby and with our new little family that I never expected what happened next.

18

Emily

Chance had just turned three weeks old when I came down from my room with him asleep in my arms. We had a new guest in the house. I didn't pay much attention to him right away as guests were becoming more frequent around here and let's be honest, I was exhausted being a new mom. I rounded the corner of the kitchen bar to see Tate sitting there. I let out an ear-piercing scream. It was so loud it woke Chance up and he started to cry.

Reader must have heard me. He came running out of his room.

"What's wrong? Is the baby okay?"

He grabs him out of my arms and tries to soothe him since I was just standing there frozen, staring at Tate.

Reader looks between me and Tate confused.

"Emily. Good to see you're well." Tate greets me.

"Emily, who is this guy?" Reader asked clearly confused.

There's silence for a while before Tate speaks again.

"Why don't you tell him who I am Emily."

"I... I... I don't know you." I whisper.

He laughs.

"Yes, you do. Tell the truth Emily."

"Sir, I don't know what is going on, but you are clearly making Emily and the baby upset."

Chance is still screaming.

Tate looks at Reader.

"You mean my baby?"

Reader looks at me in shock. I know what this looks like. Tate is much older than me. But that's not it.

I didn't notice that I had started to cry. Tears were now rolling down my cheeks.

"Why are you here?" I yell.

I'm angry now and not caring if I'm upsetting anyone.

"Why? I want to see my boy." he smiles.

Reader turns the baby just enough so that he is facing him.

"There, take a good look. Do you see him? That's what you want? Now go, leave us alone. We're good here."

He looks at him quietly while we all watch. Unaffected. Then he turns back to me.

"You know this isn't what we wanted. This wasn't the plan. This was never in the plans."

"Yeah well, this is how it went, and you don't have to be here. Nobody is asking anything from you." Reader states clearly angry also.

"See... it's kind of hard to ignore now, isn't it?

A thought flashed through my mind.

"How did you find us?"

"I want to hold him."

"No!" Reader yells.

Tate doesn't take his eyes off me.

"Emily, I want to hold my son."

"How did you find us?" I whispered.

I wanted to know.

"Let me hold him and I'll tell you."

"No way man, just fucking tell her."

Tate looks at Reader.

"This isn't really your business, is it?"

Reader looks like he's about to lose it. It takes everything I have to allow this, but I do. I want to know how he found us.

I walked over to Reader and asked him for the baby.

"Are you sure." he whispers.

I shake my head.

"Yes, I'm sure."

He hands me Chance, and I walk him over to Tate and hand Chance to him. I see an expression of tenderness wash over his face as he looks down at him. He smiles at him. Chance stops crying. This sends so much panic throughout my body that I now feel sick. Does Chance know that he's his biological father? Can he feel it? I don't want to lose this baby. Not to them. They didn't want him. They were going to get rid of him.

I shook my head in a panic at his reaction.

"No, this isn't right. You didn't want him. Neither of you wanted him. Why are you here? How did you find me?" I whisper the last part.

Tate looks up at me.

"You came through health care system. Doc let me know."

Of course, Doc!

"So what? You've changed your mind? You can't do that! You can't change your mind now! We already love him!"

I was crying again, harder than I would have liked. I hadn't noticed that Reader had come from behind me and was holding me in his arms.

"How could you change your mind?" I pleaded.

"Alicia is the one who is all caught up in what everyone else thinks. I am to a certain point but not like her. This is what she wanted, what would make her happy. You would carry the baby for her, we would pay you for it, and we would finally have our son. A son to pass our family's wealth down to. That was the plan. You know this. The plan wasn't for you to run off with our baby and call him your own Emily."

Reader pulls away from me.

"Wait a minute. He's not your baby?"

I turn and look him in the eyes, unable to speak.

"He doesn't know?" Tate asks.

"I... I... I was going to tell you..."

Reader throws his arms up in the air and laughs. But it's not a good kind of laugh.

"How can this be happening?"

I don't think he meant it as a real question but more of a statement. I turned back to Tate.

"You can't take him back!" I yelled.

"You didn't want him. You were going to end the pregnancy!"

He clears his throat.

"We weren't Emily."

"Yes, you were! Don't lie!"

"Emily, we would have never followed through."

I started shaking my head.

"No... no... no! You can't say that now. You were."

"We weren't Emily." he repeats.

"Hold up." Reader interrupts.

"Let me see if I have this right. You and your wife paid Emily to carry your child for you and when you found out your baby had Down Syndrome, you were going to end the pregnancy. But now you are saying you weren't. Emily thought you were, so she ran away, to here, to keep the baby alive and to call her own. But now you want him back?"

"We wouldn't have ended the pregnancy. There is no proof of that. It's just her word verse mine and her father's word. Do I need to explain why I would win?"

My heart stinks. *Why is he doing this? Why now?*

Lily was not home when this conversation happened. I was grateful for that. She was already very suspicious of me. I don't want to do anything now that would cause me to lose the home I've found here. I wouldn't have anywhere else to go. Not quickly.

I didn't know how long Tate was staying for. He held his baby a few times, other than that he was mostly distant. Working a lot and watching, creepily watching. I don't think Lily ever caught on about who he really was. I thought for sure Reader would tell her, but it seems that he hadn't.

With Tate here, Reader was also distant. He wasn't acting like he had been acting the last three weeks. Not like the *father figure* he was so hoping to become, I was so hoping he'd be. Everything was going so well, and now it's all messed up. Tate could take Chance, and I wouldn't be able to stop him.

"How long are you planning to be here?"

I only asked because I was curious about how much time I had left. He knew I was nursing Chance, and I felt like that was the only thing keeping him with me. Tate was seated on the couch in the living room looking through one of the books from the book shelf when I entered the room.

"That's actually what I wanted to talk to you about. Can you sit for a minute please?"

I sat down like he asked in a chair across from him. I waited for him to speak because I was too nervous to say anything else.

"I actually didn't come here to take our baby away from you."

This shocked me.

"You didn't?"

Then anger seeped in.

"Then why did you come?" I yelled.

"Calm down Emily. I will admit, I never expected you to run away with him. That was a very bold move. But I can understand why you did."

"Okay."

"I can also understand what kind of man your father is, and I don't think he treated you very well. He didn't give you the money, did he?"

I shake my head.

"He did not."

"I didn't think so."

"I took some of it when I left, that's how I got here."

"Good."

If he's not here to take the baby, then why is he here?

"Why all this then? Why come here and scare me and make me worry if you were never going to take Chance away from me?"

"I don't know. I guess I needed to know he was loved and that he would be okay with you and not around your father. If I took him back, Alicia would never love him like you would. He would be raised by the help and even I know that's not fair to a child. He would grow to be a very troubled adult and with him having special needs... well Alicia isn't really a nice woman, I will admit. As a matter of fact, she doesn't know that I am here. She hasn't asked about the baby, she acts like you both never existed. I'm going to tell her when I get back that the baby died at birth. She doesn't need to know anything else. She will never know the difference. Does that work for you?"

I am seated across from him, but it feels like I am floating outside of my body. *Is he for a real?* It takes me a moment to catch my thoughts.

"What about you?"

"Me? Well... I'm going to leave here soon. I'd like to have a moment with him to say goodbye first if that's alright? And I'm not going to pretend I don't care Emily. I do care. So, I'll have ways to watch him grow up. He doesn't need to know about me. Reader can be his father if he so chooses. You don't have to worry about me; I won't change my mind. I have no interest in making this thing bigger than it needs to be. I stay silent, you stay silent. I think we can agree on that part. I would hope your father wouldn't cause a problem; he doesn't have a good leg to stand on. He was just as much a part of this too. It would be very stupid of him to open his mouth now."

He pauses and it gives my brain a moment to catch up.

"I'm going to give you money to make sure he has what he needs.

NO.

"I don't want your money. We will be fine."

"I don't think that is true Emily, I know you don't have any and he will need things. Things that are expensive. He's still my child, this was my mess, take the money Emily. Oh, and all his medical bills will be paid for. I'll see to it."

"Are you sure?" I asked. Taking money from him seems like a loose end and I didn't want anything that could tie us together.

"I am sure Emily. I appreciate what you are doing now and how much you love him. I didn't expect this outcome, and I never would have wanted this to go like this, but it did and that's the facts. The best I can do now, is make sure you have the means to take care of him properly."

He stands up and takes out his wallet. He pulls out a check and hands it to me. Then he takes a few steps towards me and hugs me.

"Thank you, Emily. I'm going to say goodbye to Chance and then I'll be out of your way."

He walks out of the living room and heads up the stairs. Ten minutes later he walks out the front door.

I never moved the whole time he was up there with him, but as soon as he shut the front door I bolted up the stairs as fast as I could to check on Chance.

Reader was standing over his crib, his back to me.

"Is he okay?" I asked a little afraid and out of breath.

Reader turns and looks at me.

"He's fine. I saw him coming and I watched the whole time."

Relief washes over me as I walked over to look at my perfect sleeping little baby boy.

"Thank you, Reader." I said more timid than I wanted to. I didn't like what this has done to us.

He points to the paper in my hand.

"What's that?"

I looked down at the check that I had forgotten was in my hand.

"Oh, it's a check from Tate."

"Why?" Reader immediately fires back.

"To take care of us I guess."

Reader didn't say anything right after that, but I could tell he didn't like it.

Finally, he asks, "How much is it?"

"I don't know."

"Well look, Emily."

"Oh, okay."

I lifted my hand and opened the check.

"It's for five hundred thousand dollars."

My hand started shaking as I held all that money. I look up at Readers face, he seems resentful of it. At least that's what it felt like. He sees me shaking and switches his facial expression closing the space between us. He pulls me in for a hug.

"Does the money mean he is gone?" he asked.

I exhale. "I guess so."

He squeezes me harder.

"Good. Cash the check. I don't think he will come back."

"You don't?"

"No."

He pulls back and looks me in the eyes.

"I'm going to take a walk. I'm happy for you Emily."

Then he walks away, leaving me alone in my room with my check and a sleeping Chance.

19

Reader

I headed down to the stream. I have a secret spot I go to that I haven't even told Emily about. It's a place that my mother found and shared with me. She told me that my father didn't even know about it. I didn't plan on telling Emily about it and when Chance is old enough to keep a secret, I will show it to him. It'll be our thing. Only for us.

It's a little hole in the side of the riverbank that's under some thick tree roots with a giant Sycamore cascading tall above it. It's more roots than tree which makes it more unique looking. It's not huge but big enough for two people to tuck inside. Today I sit in it alone for the first time since before my parents died.

Learning that the baby wasn't Emily was wild. This whole thing is just wild. It's the kind of thing that never happens. It actually seems very impossible. But it's true. Absolutely true. I witnessed it myself.

Even though I am shocked over the entire situation, I am the most upset with Emily for not telling me. How could she lie to me? I am Chance's father. The one that actually wants to be. And Emily didn't think that this giant piece of information, this shocking truth, was something I should know being that I was more than willing to… I did put my name on Chance's birth certificate even though I'm not legally his biological father. She should have told me what she did and why. No matter the details of the situation, I should have been told. I would have supported her regardless. I would have been surprised, but I would have understood why she did what she did. Tate looks like an arrogant asshole. He paid off his surrogate to keep his "broken" child and then he is going to lie to his wife that the baby died. A child she would disown anyway. Who does that? Who even impregnates a person like he did? And her father? Scum. Disgusting. I am sick to my stomach about all of it. It's just so wild.

But Emily, she hurt me. She could have trusted me, and we could have had a plan. I would never have let Tate make a reservation with us. I would have forbidden him from our home. I could have kept him away from Chance.

Then there's Lily. Thank God she didn't find out what had happened. She is already very suspicious of Emily's intentions. This would have sent her over the edge. For Chances and Lily's safety, Lily doesn't need to know.

I'm not going to lie; the check hurt my pride. I want to be the one who takes care of them. I had every intention of being the one who saves them, in turn they are saving me. It was a perfect trade. We were giving each other a family. A clean start. Another chance at what we both lost.

But I know I need to check my pride and leave it here. Under the Sycamores and between these roots. That's why I came out here. This is where my mother and I used to work out most of our problems. If we were having a bad day, or if for some reason I was bad as a little boy and my father got upset with me, she would rush me here and we would talk through it and then leave it in the roots. I always felt better, and I always apologized to my father. He would always return my apology with a hug telling me I did the right thing. He never knew that my mom was coaching me from this secret spot we ran off to all the time.

That check, it will help Chance and give him and Emily a better life. Emily deserves that as well. She deserves her own money. I have money from my parents, and I get money monthly from their book sales, even now after they are gone, but Emily having her own money, even if it is from that awful man, is in the best interest for them both and frankly she deserves it for what Tate and her father put her through.

So, I will leave my selfish concerns here and when I head back home, I will work on not being so upset. It'll be hard, but I'll try.

20

Emily

After Tate left, we both tried to resume to normal but it was difficult. I don't think Reader trusted me anymore. Luckily, Lily didn't catch on to who Tate really was in the three days that he was here. I didn't want her to know or at least not yet. I could only handle one person's judgment at a time, and it felt like Reader was judging me for this. I was still recovering from the labor and delivery and taking care of a baby at eighteen wasn't exactly easy. I am sure it's not easy at any age, but for me... this was not what I was supposed to be doing. I was supposed to be living my life for me, not for a child. But he has special needs, and I wanted to wholeheartedly give him everything he would need. A life he deserved. Maybe I am spoiling him by not letting him cry and holding him too much, but I can't look at his little face and deny him this care. He's lucky to be alive. I feel lucky to have him. I don't care what Tate says, he wouldn't be here or loved this much if it wasn't for me.

It felt like Reader and I were only on speaking terms if it had to do with Chance. I tried to have a conversation with him after Tate left but he said it wasn't a good time for him. He would let me know when he was ready to talk. I decided to drop it until then. But I missed him. Deeply.

I thought that once we got into our new routine that we would still sneak off and lay under the tall trees and he would read to me again. I thought that we would still live our lives like the teenagers that we still were. I thought that we were still falling in love.

Keeping the full truth from him hurt him more than I realized it would. I had my reasons though. To be honest I don't know if I would have ever told him if it had not come out on its own. I have a hard time trusting people and I don't really trust love. I've never had a reason to trust it. This secret was big. It was so big that if it came out the wrong way it could have altered all our lives forever. I don't think I could ever stomach this baby being taken away from me. I would never recover. My heart would never recover. I had to do what I did for him. I know Reader said he wanted to be his father on the birth certificate, but just because he signed it, I still couldn't trust that completely. I really hope when the hurt subsides a bit, he understands why I had to keep it all to myself.

But our new normal only lasted a week. For reasons I couldn't quite figure out, Chance was crying a lot. And from what I read, it is not a normal amount.

Reader popped his head into my room one morning.

"It's been four days Emily. Do you think we should get him to the doctor and get him checked out?"

I'm lying on my bed with Chance on my chest. He's just finished nursing but is back to crying again. Just little sobs, enough to break my heart. A tear rolls down my cheek and I know Reader catches it, he says nothing. I say nothing. He takes my silence as a yes.

"I'll give the doc a call and let you know what time he can see him. Do you want me to take him for a while so you can get up and get ready."

I take a deep breath; nothing feels like it should. Reader wanted to be Chances dad, but he doesn't feel like it. I feel like he's helping me out of pity now. Which feels awful.

"Sure, thank you."

I lift Chance off my chest and hand him over to Reader. He's still crying.

"If he's too much, you can bring him back."

Reader nods.

"Em, take your time. Take a bath or grab a shower. I know he hasn't been easy the last few days, but I can handle him. Take the time for you, we both know that you need it."

He doesn't wait for me to reply; he just turns and walks away. I know he means it, so I get up and make myself a warm bath.

The water soothes me. I haven't had a bath since a few days after giving birth, to relieve my soreness after the birth. Things just got busy, and I guess I got obsessed with Chances care instead of taking time for my own. Reader must notice it too. I don't think he is judging me, but him still being upset with me makes me feel like it's judgment. I need to find a way for him to forgive me. I wish he would talk to me.

I spent the next twenty minutes racking my brain as to how to do that. I came up with nothing.

I get out of the tub and dry off then walk back to my room. Reader had left a note on my bed.

"I got him to sleep in his little bassinet, doctor's appointment this afternoon at two. Take your time Em."

Even when he is mad at me, he is still nice. He had also left breakfast on my nightstand and a book under the note.

I dress quickly and brush through my hair. I don't care as much about my appearance as I do about starting this book he brought up. It's not a book of poetry. It's another one of his mother's novels. I flipped it over and read the back. It's a story about forgiveness and letting go. Which confuses me because I don't need to forgive him for anything, in fact it's the other way around. I need him to forgive me.

But he must have given me the book for a reason, and I am open to finding out why. I lay back and open it up. I am immediately sucked into the story. It's a young love story that feels familiar to me or at least how I thought I was feeling with Reader.

Two hours went by fast. I didn't even realize it until I heard a knock on my door. Reader peeked his head in. He had Chance in his arms.

"Hey."

"Hey, how's the book?" he whispers.

I inserted the bookmark that he put in the book for me inside the page I was on so later I could pick up where I left off.

"It's really good Reader! I lost track of time I guess. Is he hungry?"

"Yeah, he's stirring so I thought I'd get him up here before he starts wailing."

He smiles but we both know that it's not all that funny.

"Okay, thank you."

"Of course. So, we should probably leave here about one so there's enough time to get through traffic. Will that work?"

I look at the clock on my wall. It's noon.

"Yes, that will work."

"Okay. Great! Hopefully it's nothing, I would hate it to be something but at least something is an answer, you know?"

I read the concern on his face.

"Yes, I get that. He can't just be crying for no reason. That doesn't seem right."

"It doesn't. But what do we really know, first time parents and all?"

His words caught me off guard and I thought I saw a gleam in his eye. He smiles.

I smile back at him and soak in the first normal *us* moment we've had since Tate showed up.

He breaks the moment by bringing over Chance and putting him in my arms.

"I can come back up in a bit to help you get ready if you need me too?" he asks.

I shake my head no.

"That's okay, I'll be down after I feed him. Maybe grab a bite to eat first."

"I'll make you a sandwich."

He walks out of my room closing the door behind him.

I'm in shock at how nice he is to me, not believing I fully deserve it.

21

Emily

Nursing Chance has become the biggest joy for me. Something I had never expected to love. Something I never expected to do. Is it weird to nurse a baby that biologically isn't yours? I should stop thinking that way. He is mine. I think he was meant to be mine from the beginning. I know it in my soul. I feel it. He is mine.

I'm not going to lie; I was nervous about my mothering instincts kicking in. I shouldn't have been. They are in full force. I feel connected to Chance, and I feel very protective. I'll never let anything, or anyone hurt him. Not if I can help it.

He looks a little different in the eyes from other babies I've seen. I know he's going to continue to look more and more different than the other kids around him, but I will do what I must do to make sure he's a happy boy, with a happy life, even if that means sheltering him a little. I don't want to, but I can already feel the anxiety brewing in me of the possible issues that could arise from his specific needs. It will kill me to see other kids make fun of him.

Aside from his beautiful brown eyes looking a little different, which I think makes him cuter, he has the cutest little button nose and light brown hair. A thin layer. It's the same color as mine, which I love that we match. He also has very chunky cheeks. Part of me is a little happy that I can't see his parents in his face. Selfishly I think that would just make it harder for me. What matters most is that I think he is perfect and that he's going to be deeply loved.

The doctor's appointment wasn't much help. There's nothing wrong with him. Appearance wise he's perfectly healthy. They called him *possibly colicky*. A term I read about in one of my baby books. The doctors' advice was to try swaddling. Something we haven't done yet and I guess it is something most babies love.

I asked Reader if we could stop at a baby store to grab one. He insisted that he knew where one was at the house.

Chance fell asleep in his car seat on the way home. He was out cold, so we decided to just let him sleep in his seat until he woke up. I wasn't really in the mood to listen to him cry *for no reason*. I was still frustrated and also skeptical that the doctor's appointment was even helpful.

Reader set him down in the living room where it was quiet.

"Follow me."

His words caught me off guard because I didn't have any idea what he meant. When I hesitated, he walked back over to me and grabbed my hand.

"Come on Em."

"Where are we going?"

"Up to the attic."

Okay. What's in the attic?

Chance Worth Taking

Reader led me back towards his room. This was the first time I had seen it. For as long as I've been here, he's been very private about his space. Sometimes I still feel like a guest, even after Lily and Reader refused to let me pay to stay here after the first month. *Guests didn't go into the owner's wing of the house.* That's what I was told. So I never did. Maybe things are changing. Maybe this will feel more like my home one day and Chances too. I wanted that more than anything.

His room was tidy. Very blue. Dark Blue bedding and curtains to match. He had a bookshelf also. I imagine they were books he didn't want other people to see or touch. Or maybe to know about. Maybe they were his parents' books. Either way I didn't ask about them. On his dresser was a photo of him with his parents. I stopped as I passed to have a closer look. He looked just like his momma. I sometimes wonder why I couldn't look more like my momma. I look like my father and I hate it. I want to look in the mirror and see my momma's face.

The attic was behind a door that was in the corner of his room. He opened it and we headed up a very long, two-story set of stairs. When we reached the top, it was clear that the attic was as big as the whole house. It was gigantic. Bigger than the house I lived in with my father.

"Wow this is amazing Reader! And clean for an attic. Look how organized this stuff is?" I joked but was also amazed.

From what I know which isn't much, attics are supposed to be messy, dusty, cobwebby, creepy, and cluttered. At least that's how they are in the movies.

He starts walking all the way to the back, so I follow him.

"I remembered at the doctor's office that my mother kept a tote of my brothers' things. She donated most of it because she knew a family in our community that needed it, but she kept a few things. One of the things was a hand-made swaddle blanket that one of Lily's church ladies made. It has our last name on it, that's why she didn't give it away."

Reader moves a few boxes and uncovers a little tote. He opens the tote and digs through a few things that look like clothes. Then he pulls out a light blue blanket.

"Here it is."

He holds it open to show me how it works. It's got Velcro that wraps around and attaches to the back, so it gets nice and tight. His last name was embroidered on the front. *Whitmore.*

I loved it.

"That's cool. I really hope it works."

"Me too. We can take this tote downstairs and use whatever we need out of it. It's not doing anyone any good up here. I'm sure my mother would want us to use this stuff if we could."

He digs through the tote and holds up a few outfits for me to see. Cute ones. There are a couple more personalized blankets and some room decorations. Which I had not thought about since we shared a room. But maybe I will use them. It would be a nice touch for his side of the room. Making it more baby-ish.

Reader pulls the tote out of its spot and begins to put the other boxes back in its place. While he's doing that one of the boxes tips over and a few books and pictures fall out.

I bent down to pick it up while he's holding the tote in his hands. At the same time we both hear Chance crying.

"I got this, you grab him, and I'll catch up."

"Okay. Thanks."

While reader headed to the attic door, I scooped up the pictures that had fallen out of the box. I was naturally curious, so I looked at them before putting them back away.

They were pictures of a girl. She was young, had strawberry blond hair and was as thin as a pencil. As I flipped through them quickly, she appeared to be between the age of five and maybe fifteen. I flipped one of them over to see if there was a date, there wasn't. Instead, there was name... *Poppy* and a description... *age sixteen, Isle of Palms, Summer Vacation.* It was a picture of her standing in the ocean splashing waves at the camera. She looked happy.

I scooped the rest of the pictures up and put them back in the box. Also on the floor was what looked like a small diary. A locked one. It had Poppy's name written on the cover.

I could still hear Chance crying, and I figured I was out of time before Reader came back up to get me. I shoved the diary and the picture along with another one in the back of my pants. I closed the lid to the box and headed back downstairs.

Reader met me at the bottom of the stairs.

"I think he's hungry."

"Yeah, he probably is." I said as calmly as I could so that I didn't seem off.

Reader handed Chance and the swaddle to me and I headed up to my room to feed him and to read Poppy's diary, now very curious because Poppy was my momma's name.

22

Emily

Chance has fallen back to sleep while nursing. He took forever though. This was the first time since he was born that I wanted him to hurry. Only because I wanted to read the diary.

I was extremely confused. Either Lily's daughter coincidentally had the same unique name as my momma, or Lily's daughter *was* my momma. The latter probably is a long shot. Either way I had to know what was in this diary and I couldn't wait any longer.

I spent a few minutes getting Chance swaddled. It was easy to do once I relaxed and thought about it. Lucky for me he seemed to be content in it. I strapped him in his swing and rushed back over to my bed to try to open the diary.

It had one of those childish locks on it. It was in the shape of a heart. I looked over at my nightstand for the knife I left in my room from yesterday's lunch. It was still there. It was a butter knife, but I had faith that it would still do the job. I used it to pry open the diary. Not the lock but the bindings that held the lock. The cover was made of heavy cardboard, and it was quite easy to pry the metal hooks out of it that held the lock on.

Once I got it, I tossed the lock aside and opened the diary up. The first thing I read was: *This diary belongs to Poppy...*

December 22nd, 1979

To my baby. Nobody knows about you yet. But I do. I can feel you growing inside me. I woke up this morning and I just knew you were there. Alive. Your father and I were a bit careless about a month or so ago. But I'm not upset. I love you already. I'm not sure how long I am going to keep you a secret. I'm still not old enough to make all my own decisions and my mother is extremely strict, especially since my father died last year. She's on top of me about everything. My father would have loved you like I do though. He was great like that! I have to find out if your daddy will be happy about you as well. I'm not sure yet because we have only been going steady for a couple of months. I need to finish high school and graduate so that I can be properly educated for you. Give you a good life. I will be about seven months along with you when that happens so I'm not sure how that will go. I turn eighteen in July. If my calculations are correct, you will be born sometime in the beginning of August. So please wait until I am eighteen and don't come early on your own time. I need to make sure I am old enough so that I get to make all your decisions. All our decisions.

I am in love with you already and I haven't even met you yet. That's so crazy!

Love, Your Momma XOXO

December 24th, 1979

It's Christmas Eve and I have all I need this year for Christmas. You! I wanted to be asking for presents for you instead of for me, but I can't let anyone know yet that you are inside me. I'm afraid they will try to talk me into not keeping you. I am going to tell your father tomorrow when I see him. He's promised to take me to see the Christmas lights. I love looking at everyone's houses all lit up for the holiday. Someday we are going to have our own big house to light up. It will be so bright, you'd be able to see it from space! We have so many amazing things to look forward to. I want to do them all with you! I've been singing Christmas carols to you; can you hear them? Probably not, but I like to think you can. I will sing them to you when you can hear them.

I love you sweet baby!

Love, Momma. XOXO

December 25th, 1979

Little Baby. Merry Christmas. It's technically your first Christmas. You have a heartbeat so it counts, and you are here with me, that's all I can think about. We ate Christmas ham your Grammy Lily cooked and my favorite mashed potatoes with gravy. We ate a lot of it. I don't want you to starve! I also want you to get used to Christmas dinners. It was a little sad without my daddy there. Next year you will be eating with us. You will only be about four months old, but I know by then you will love to sit with us at the table. Maybe next year won't have to be so sad after all.

Your daddy didn't take me to see the Christmas lights tonight. His parents got into a huge fight, and he had to sort that out instead. I don't think they are very good people. They fight a lot. We might decide that you won't know them. Just to keep you safe. You don't need anyone in your life that doesn't keep you safe. Always remember that. Always remember I will always keep you safe! I always will or I'll die trying.

So because of that mess, I didn't get to tell him about you tonight like I wanted to. I wanted to give him good news but not on a day where he was dealing with bad news. So we will wait for another time. A better time. Maybe New Years. A New Year's resolution you can be. A fresh start.

I love you!

Love, Momma XOXO

December 31, 1979

Baby Love. I told your father about you tonight. I thought he would want to ring in the New Year the three of us. I thought he would be ecstatic to begin new. Just us. He could leave his horrible family and start a new life with us. Maybe even my mother would take us all in. I'm sure she will love you just as fast as I did once I tell her. I'm hoping she does. You deserve a happy, loving family.

But the news didn't go so well. He was upset. He said he wouldn't know how to raise a child because he can't even keep his own family straight.

He said no. We're not doing this and if I wanted to keep you, I would have to do it on my own. Then he dropped me off at home and left.

But you know what? I'm not upset. This isn't what I was hoping for, but I still have you and you are all I want and need anyways. I don't need anything else but you and my mother if she will still have me. If not, then all I need is you! Tomorrow we will think of a new plan. Just us. We will think of the greatest plan!

Happy New Year Baby Love! I love you the most!

Love, Your Momma. XOXO

February 07, 1980

Baby Girl. It's been a rough month. Morning sickness and all that. I plan on telling your grandmother Lily about you at dinner. It's getting harder to hide you since I started showing and it is the end of our first trimester. I think it might be time to go see a doctor, but I can't do that without a parent with me. I'm hoping this goes well. I will be right back, and I will tell you how it went, even though I'm positive you will hear the whole thing anyways. I'll be right back.

Love, Momma XOXO

P.s, I can tell you are a girl.

Lorinda Faye

February 09, 1980

Hi Love. I'm sorry I didn't get right back to you when I said I was going too. If you can hear at all, I wouldn't have to owe you an explanation. It didn't go well and it's been a couple of terrible days. I've spent most of them crying. My mother, your grandmother Lily, is upset with me. She doesn't know how I could be so irresponsible and embarrassing. My father and her didn't raise me to be so reckless with my life and to get pregnant by such a low-class man. I have a feeling she is going to try to send me away. Maybe to live with a relative of ours. Someone who can "handle me" better than she can. She doesn't know how I "could do this" to her. I don't know what to do or who to turn to. I'm going to have to think of something. But don't worry, I will. It's going to be alright.

I love you my little love.

Love, Your Momma XOXO

February 14, 1980

Hey baby girl. Today is a very special day for me. It's Valentine's Day. It's my favorite holiday ever. I don't have a "Valentine" this year, so I de-cided it was going to be YOU. We can celebrate it together. When you are old enough, I'm going to make Valentine's Day so much fun for us! I can't wait!

Extra XOXOXOXO's baby girl,
Love, Momma XOXO

March 21, 1980
Hey Baby Love,
Everyone at school knows about you. You're hard to hide. Mother is not happy. She's "never been more embarrassed." And your daddy, he hasn't been around at all since I told him about you. I heard a rumor that his parents weren't good and he had to drop out. I don't know what's going on there. But it must be bad. Some of the popular kids are making fun of me. But you know what, I don't care. I don't. I have you and that's all I care about. I don't care if my mother is mad at me forever. It's her loss. As soon as I turn eighteen we will just go away and be on our own. I don't know how yet but I will figure it out. I've got to go love. I have a test to study for.

Love, Your Momma XOXO

April 10, 1980

I felt you kick today! Like hard! It was the great-est feeling ever! It made me so happy. It feels like you are in a boxing match in there. You probably are! I can just picture what you look like. I bet you are cute as a button! No offense to your daddy but I hope you look like me. I was a really cute baby.

Anyways, Love you my precious baby! You're getting so big!

Love, Momma XOXO

June 20, 1980

Sorry I haven't written in a while. I've been so busy growing you and also finishing my studies. I needed to make sure I graduated high school so I can get a good job and take care of you. Final ex-ams were hard but guess what! We did it! And we graduated too! I have my certificate and everything.

Your Grammy has come around a little and she took me to the doctor's office, and I got to hear your heartbeat! It was so amazing. The doctor told me you were a boy, but I don't believe him. I know you are a girl. Only six more weeks and we get to meet. I couldn't be more excited. Grammy Lily has

already started buying you things. I think she's going to love you just as much as I do.

It's almost time love!

See you soon,

Love, Momma XOXO

July 4, 1980

It's my birthday baby girl. We did it! I am officially eighteen. Officially an adult. Grammy and
I got into a big fight tonight. It was about you. She's
worried about the quality of life I will give you
raising a baby with no job and no money. My
daddy left us in an okay place, but it will make
it harder when there's a baby in the picture. I
don't know what to do. She said the hospital bills
alone will drain our savings. I feel bad, but it's
for you. How can anyone argue over that? Anyways
it's left me in a sour mood. I'm supposed to be
happy right now. It's my birthday! All I want now
is you... I'm ready if you are?

Can't wait to meet you sweet, sweet girl!

Love, Your Momma XOXO

Lorinda Faye

Aug 3, 1980

The contractions have started baby girl. I think tonight or tomorrow is going to be the day. You're finally coming. These pains are bad though. You hurt. But I don't care. Momma's still mad at me but by tomorrow she won't be. I just know it. Ouch! Okay, I have to go. I'm going to tell her I'm ready. You're ready I love it so much!

See you very soon baby girl!

Love, Momma XOXO

23

Emily

I took another look at the photo of a young Poppy then I closed the diary. That's all that was written in it. There's nothing else. Nothing from after the birth of her baby. And no more clues leading to Poppy being my momma. This baby and I didn't have the same birthday. Mine is October 15th. And my name is Emily. So as much as I was hoping, this diary probably wasn't written by my momma.

I shove it under my mattress. I don't want Reader to know that I have it. Or Lily. I'm not sure if she has even seen it. It's possible she has, but I don't have any business reading it or taking it in the first place especially without permission. I would be extremely embarrassed if I got caught with it. I will try to return it as soon as I get the chance.

Lily was in the kitchen getting dinner ready when I came back downstairs with Chance. She turns and smiles at us.

"He looks happier."

"Yes, he does, doesn't he? I definitely think he slept better all swaddled up. I don't know for sure, but that thing might be the answer we were looking for. I'm really hoping."

"That's good to hear dear. He sure does have a set of lungs on him."

I wanted to laugh but I also knew it wasn't that funny. I immediately started to apologize.

"I am so sorry he's been such a fuss. I feel bad. I came here and I feel like I've just disrupted your lives."

Lily turns from the stove.

"Emily, you and Chance are not a disrupt. I quite enjoy you here. You've been a blessing. Both of you. Even if it is noisy."

She nods her head once and turns back to the stove. I feel better that she said that, but it also makes me feel sad for her. Sad because we must remind her of her daughter and the grandchild that she lost. Maybe that's why she enjoys having us around. Maybe it's a good thing.

I spent all of dinner distracted thinking about what I read in Poppy's diary and feeling bad for Lily. I was dying to know the rest of the story. I kept going through different scenarios in my head about what could have possibly happened. I think Readers' books were influencing me to think these wild and elaborate stories about what could have happened to her. Reader even noticed my lack of participation at dinner.

"You okay Em?" he asked after I had put Chance down for the night. We had started making it a habit again to meet back in the living room or out by the trees, which was a huge relief. Reader got me this special baby monitor that could reach a longer distance so I could feel comfortable being so far away from the house. But tonight, we were in the living room since the rain started up a few hours ago.

"Yes, why?"

"I don't know. Seems like you've got something on your mind. Care to share?"

I felt like it would be weird to just ask questions out of the blue, but I wanted to know and he asked.

"Umm... I guess, for some reason I have been thinking about Lily and her daughter. I feel sad for her I guess."

Reader scratches his head. He does that a lot when he thinks. I find it ridiculously cute.

"Yeah, it's pretty sad. There's been a lot of death in both our lives. Even though Lily lost her daughter and grand-daughter years ago, it's like sometimes their presence is still around. I know Lily feels it. Just like I feel my parents' presence."

He pauses for a second before he adds, "You know, she told me about a week ago that she feels them around more since you and the baby showed up. I think that's why she likes you guys here. I think she feels closer to her daughter and granddaughter. I don't know, it's kind of weird."

His words shocked me.

"Weird how?" I look at him intensely wanting to know what he means.

"I don't know. One minute she's kind of on the fence about you and then the next she doesn't want you to leave and you're both a blessing."

"Uh huh." I take a moment to think about how I want to ask him about Poppy.

"Reader, what all do you know about her daughter. I've been so curious?"

Reader reclines back in his chair, flipping out the footrest. He's laid all the way back, looking up at the ceiling now. I have the strongest urge to throw my body onto his. I want to know what that would feel like in the worst way. I resist because, well I'm terrified to actually do it, but also, he looks like he's going to tell me about Poppy.

"I know her name was Poppy and my mom used to babysit her when she was little for Lily and Bill. That was Lily's husband's name. I don't know if you knew that."

"No, I didn't. So, your mom was a lot older that Poppy?"

"Yeah, about ten years older. She was her sitter until she was about twelve. My mom used to talk about Poppy a lot. They were close and that's how she knew she wanted to be a mother, because she had so much practice with Poppy. Anyways, my mom said when she hit fifteen, she fell into a rebellious stage pretty hard. Causing a lot of grief for Lily and Bill. And before you ask, no, that is not why Bill had a heart attack. Lily was too good of a cook and Bill wasn't exactly a healthy size. He didn't take good care of himself. From what my mom said, Poppy had Bill wrapped around her finger. Which made Lily more infuriated. My mom said Poppy got away with too much because of it. He died a few days before Poppy's sixteenth birthday."

"Oh my gosh! How devastating. Lily has had a lot of loss around her also, hasn't she?"

"Yep, and it's just her and I left."

I felt like he might have finished talking about Poppy, but I wanted him to talk about her more. I wanted to know if he knew anything about a baby.

"Can you tell me about when Poppy died... unless you don't want too?"

I didn't want to sound too desperate, but my curiosity was killing me.

"I know she left home at some point, and I know she came back later in an urn. Both Poppy and her daughter came back. That's those two urns on the fireplace. That's all I know. My mother didn't tell me about that part. I think it was out of respect for Lily or to protect me maybe. Lily was devastated and my mother was the only one who could console her. I was only five at that time, so I barely remember any of it. I just remember my mother crying. I think it hurt her a lot more than she wanted anyone to know. It hurt her to see Lily hurting, but from what I've gathered on my own, I think there's a piece to this puzzle missing. A big one. Things felt weird to me. Like how it all went down. But I wouldn't know what that was. I was young myself. We talked about them from time to time but like I said, my mother was very hush about it."

I took all that in. There was a lot to think about. At some point Poppy must have left with her baby. But something happened after that, a reason, or an explanation to why they both didn't make it.

Reader is still laid back in his chair, but his eyes are closed now. He looks so peaceful. I don't want to interrupt his peace, but this is the best we have gotten along in a while. It even feels like he's not upset with me anymore. I take this time to say something that's been on my mind since Tate left.

"Reader?"

He takes a few seconds to reply.

"Yeah."

"I um... I wanted to thank you for everything you've done for Chance and me since he was born. And since I came here."

He doesn't open his eyes but responds.

"It's not a problem, Em."

"Yeah, I know, but please let me finish. It's a big deal to me. I know my... my situation was unexpected. Okay, very shocking and you've still been so kind to me and so great with Chance. I never wanted to lie to you. I just didn't know how to tell you what I did."

He sits up and closes the footrest on his chair.

"Did you think that I would judge you somehow or worse, turn you in?"

He looks slightly upset, sad even.

I shake my head.

"No, not at all. It's just... I don't know. I was scared... embarrassed... I just needed to protect Chance at all costs. I had too."

"Em look at me please."

I lifted my eyes to his.

"I understand."

"You do."

"Yes."

Relief washes over me with lightning speed and I start crying.

"I'm so sorry Reader... I'm so sorry."

He gets up from his chair and within seconds he's holding me in his arms.

"I know Em. And I'm sorry too. I didn't need to get that upset over it. I could have chosen to understand why you didn't tell me. All I did was put this wedge between us."

He's got my face in his hands now and he's wiping my tears with his thumbs.

"Em." I look up into his eyes.

He smiles.

"Can we knock out that wedge?"

I smile back but the tears still fall. He kisses them, one cheek at a time.

And then he kisses me.

24

Emily

Reader spent the night in my bed with me. I still can't believe that was real. I wanted someone to pinch me to see if I was dreaming. Feeling his arms around me was a very close second to holding Chance. The best part was that I felt complete for the first time in my life. I had everything I wanted. I had a real family, and I had love.

Chance had woken up twice in the middle of the night. Reader had gotten up to grab him so I could nurse him in bed. It felt good to be taken care of.

Sometime during the last feeding, we all fell asleep and when it was morning we all woke up together. I don't know if I could be any happier than at this moment. Chance was in between Reader and I but it felt like there was no space at all. I had my eyes glued on him still asleep. He must have felt me staring at him because suddenly his eyes popped open.

"Good morning." he whispers.

I felt my face get hot.

"Morning." I managed to choke out.

Reader held his eyes on mine. That was until Chance decided to make his presence known, not with a cry but with a coo and a smile.

"Oh my God, did you just see that?" Reader yells in excitement.

"I did! He just smiled!"

"I think he likes seeing us both here. Don't you? You've got both your momma and daddy. Look how happy he is."

My heart flutters... Momma and Daddy.

Reader reaches over Chance and grabs my hand with his. He interlocks our fingers and we just lay there in the happiest moment I've ever known. It lasts for about one minute before Chance's smile turns into a cry.

Reader and I both laugh.

"Guess it's time for me to get up and for Chance to eat breakfast."

"I guess so! The baby boss has spoken."

Reader rolls out of my bed and stands up.

"Want to head to the library today? We can bring the little guy. Show him off to Marianne. Maybe grab some lunch after if he's feeling it?"

"Yeah sure, why not."

Reader bends down and kisses Chance on the head then he leans towards me and kisses me quickly on the lips.

Okay, I guess that just happened... I could get used to this!

Feeding Chance was an absolute delight. I love looking down on his perfect little face. I have so much love for him, it's insane. I often think about how my father couldn't feel the same about me. I'll never understand it.

I am a bit worried about taking him out in public and people noticing that he's not like other babies. It would hurt me so much if he got picked on or worse if they felt *bad* for him. He's alive, he's perfect, and he's loved. To me that's the most important thing. I will have to work on how everyone else will make me feel.

***

It took us an hour and a half to get ready and to grab a quick breakfast before we were off to the library. Luckily it was Chances morning nap time so he wouldn't be fussy while we were out... as long as he stayed asleep.

"What kind of books are you looking to check out today." Reader asked me as he reached over and grabbed my hand to hold it.

"I was thinking of checking out some fitness books. Maybe one on yoga. I don't know... something to help take off this baby weight faster."

Reader lifts our hands to his lips and kisses the back of mine.

"I think you look amazing for just having a baby."

His compliment felt nice.

"Well thank you, that's nice of you to say but I've been given the clear from my doctor to start up my normal activities. So, I appreciate you saying I look good, but for me, I could look and feel better."

He doesn't say another word until we get to the library. He gets Chance out of the back seat, still in his car seat and carries him into the library, my hand in his.

Marianne's face lights up the second she sees us.

"Reader, wow look at him! Isn't he a doll? Aww... those chubby cheeks too!"

She looks up at Reader and winks. If she noticed he was different, she didn't say a thing.

"Tell me mom, how are you feeling?"

"I feel great, thank you!"

Mom?!

That was the first time I've heard myself called that by someone else other than Reader.

She clasps her hands.

"Excellent. I have an idea. Why don't you give me him since he's sleeping anyways. I'll take him with me behind the counter so you two can grab your books without having to tow him around."

She reaches for Chance before I can say anything. Reader just hands him over rather easily for my liking, but I didn't want to not trust his judgment, so I stayed quiet. With Chance out of my sight, I won't lie, it makes me nervous. The only good thing about Chance hanging out with Maryanne was that Reader and I got a chance to roam the library like we used to.

I picked out a couple beginner yoga books and one on post pregnancy weight loss while Reader got more poetry books.

"Don't you ever get bored reading the same thing over and over again?"

I knew he wasn't bored; I was just messing with him. My kind of flirting.

He fake laughs. Then he pushes me against the bookshelf and places his face inches from mine.

"I don't get bored with anything, and no two poems are the same."

I smile. "Oh yeah. So, you could watch a whole baseball game, all nine innings and not get bored? Or how about golf? Like a while eighteen holes. That doesn't bore you?"

He laughs.

"What? You're nuts."

He holds my eyes.

"Fine, yeah okay. I'd get bored watching baseball or golf. And it's not because I don't like those sports, I do. It's just because I can't sit down that long without falling asleep."

I giggle.

"Oh, so what we have here is a snoozer?"

I make a fake snoring noise while I laugh almost uncontrollably.

Reader takes this opportunity to kiss me.

He really kisses me.

Like take my breath away, kisses me.

When he pulls back, his eyes are glazed over.

"So, your doctor gave you the all clear?"

It took me about thirty seconds to realize what he was saying.

"Oh, umm... yeah."

He brushed back a piece of my hair that had gotten loose from behind my ear when he kissed me.

"Do you want too?"

"Right here?" I asked shocked he would ask that here.

"No. Oh my gosh, no!" he laughs. Then he leans in and kisses me again. When he pulls back, he asks, "How about tonight?"

I was still floating on my little cloud nine. But I also knew I wanted this pretty damn badly.

"Yes, please." I whisper.

Reader looks so happy. I can't help but love that for him at this moment. If anyone deserves happiness, it's him.

"Come on let's check out now."

We check out our books, grab Chance and then head across the street to eat lunch, perfectly happy in our little bubble of three.

Chance Worth Taking

***

The diner was busy but luckily for us there was one booth left. The server walked us to it, and we sat down. There were three of us this time, instead of two. I loved how this felt. We really did feel like a family. Something I didn't feel like I've ever had in my life and I was completely in love with us. I think Reader was too.

I ate a light lunch. If Reader and I were going to make love later, I didn't want to be full or bloated for our big moment together. I'm not trying to be perfect, he knows I won't be. I haven't lost much weight besides what the baby weighed. I am still fifteen or twenty pounds over what I weighed before I was impregnated with Chance. I just really didn't want to be uncomfortable because I ate a huge lunch before.

I don't have that much experience when it comes to sex or making love for that matter. I'm certain I have never *made love* before, it was just sex a few times with a couple of guys from my school and that was before I got pregnant. After that, nobody in my small town looked my way. They judged me. They assumed I just got knocked up by someone. But I didn't care. I was getting out of there after I had the baby and had my money. I was going to go very far away. But as you know already, that didn't happen exactly like that. Instead, I ran away *with* the baby.

Those guys, they weren't serious. I wanted them to be. I wanted to love and be loved back, but nobody really wanted to date the poor girl. The girl who lived in a shitty trailer, who doesn't have a mom, and her father was only a low-class, low-income groundskeepers for the richest family in the county. So those relationships, they never lasted long and the only reason they lasted as long as they did, I was told, was because I was pretty and thin and I "put out." I wasn't easy. I just wanted to be loved. I wanted to know what that felt like. It wasn't love then, but now I know and I love how love felt so far.

I wonder how many women Reader has slept with. I wonder if I asked if he would tell me? I wonder if there was ever anyone serious. I know there was the one that was Chad's ex-girlfriend. I wonder if they had sex. I'm sure they did. I shouldn't worry about this.

As I was thinking about it, Chad and his friends passed our booth. But instead of heading towards the door, Chad turned towards us, his friends mimicking him like they did when we saw them before. I knew in my gut that this wasn't going to end well.

25

Emily

Chad's face turns smug.

"Well, well, well if it isn't the towns newest daddy. Whatcha got their Reed? A whole ass family at nineteen, isn't that so sweet."

I look away from Chad who seems to be pleased with himself, to look at Reader. I can see his face start to turn red. He's trying to keep his cool. He pops a French fry in his mouth and doesn't acknowledge Chad at all. He's not going to react.

I look back at Chad who's now fully noticing Chance who's starting to wake. I see realization hit his face; he brings his hand to his mouth and bursts out laughing.

"Wow, you bred yourself a retard, didn't you?"

Chad quickly turns to his friends who are all laughing now, then points at Chance. This lasted all of three seconds before Reader was out of his seat shoving Chad into his friends.

"What did you call him?"

Chad, not backing down repeats himself.

"He's a retard. You fathered a retard. That's hilarious!"

I see Reader pull his arm back and then he plants his fist square on Chad's nose. Chad yells in pain.

"You fucker! What the fuck. I think you broke my nose. Chad brings his hand to his nose and when he pulls it back, blood starts running down his lip.

"What the fuck asshole." he yells so loud that we now have everyone's attention.

"Asshole? Really? I'm the asshole? Fuck you, Chad."

"Wow! Having a tard for a kid has made you sensitive." one of the other guys says while laughing.

"You want me to hit you too Ronny?"

Ronny scoffs.

"I'd like to see you try. But I don't think you want to embarrass yourself in front of the rag you knocked up."

Rag? What does that mean?

I didn't have more than a second to think about it before Reader pulls back and punches Ronny in the face too. In a blink everyone is throwing punches.

All of this had taken place in less than a few minutes and it took no time at all for someone to come over and break the fight up.

When that happened, four people were bleeding. Chad, Ronny, another guy, and Reader. And everyone was thrown out, for good.

I watched Chad and his friends leave the diner. Then I turn to look at Reader.

He was bleeding from his forehead. It looked like his head was split open.

"Oh my God. Your head is cut wide open!"

"Yeah, it feels like it."

"Well should we get to the emergency room?" I asked with concern.

"No." he says sharply.

"No?"

"No, we gotta go. Grab Chance and let's go home."

He pulls cash out of his pocket and throws it down on the table. That's when I notice his hand is all bloody too. It looks like his knuckles are cut wide open as well.

"Reader we really should go to the hospital."

He makes eye contact with me now. He sees my concern and softens his tone.

"I'll go but I'm not going with you two. Chance needs to get home and so do you. I'm not bringing him to that germ filled place."

"Oh, okay."

Smart.

He takes Chance, who is still in his car seat now fully awake, out of my hands. I resisted letting him take him because I didn't want him to hurt his hand more by carrying him and I really didn't want blood on Chances stuff.

"I've got him Emily. Can we please just go?"

"Sure."

That was all I could say. Our perfect day now ruined by Chad and his idiot friends and Chances first time being called that horrible word. I felt sick to my stomach.

***

We pulled into the house fifteen minutes later. Reader got out, opened the door for me like he always does, then got Chance out.

"I'm not going to go in. I don't want Lily to see me like this."

I nodded. Only because I felt like I had no say in his decision. Once we reached the top of the steps, he handed

Chance to me who was cooing and smiling like it was just a normal day.

"I guess I better get in and feed him. Good luck."

Words felt awkward right now. Everything felt off and I don't know what he's thinking.

"I'll be back soon."

"Okay."

I took Chance into the house and headed straight upstairs. I didn't want to risk seeing Lily and having to explain to her what happened. I'd rather leave that for Reader to do.

Chance's crying has gotten remarkably better since we started swaddling him. He's like a whole new baby. He's also getting super chunky. In just a few days he is going to be two months old. It's crazy how fast time goes by.

Life before him... life before the pregnancy seemed so far behind me. Like it was another lifetime ago. When in reality, it was only about a year ago.

A lot has changed. I've changed. I'm guessing Readers changed. A baby really does change your whole life and under our circumstances, it feels like the change is exponential for all of us.

But time now, it flies. Almost two whole months have gone by feeding him around the clock, changing his diapers, and singing him to sleep.

This was never how I planned my life to go. It was never how I imagined it. I didn't really imagine too much anyways. Small towns and toxic people will do all they can to keep you small with them. They never grow personally, and they will distract you from dreaming of something bigger.

I don't have a whole lot of memories of my momma, but I have the faintest memory of her talking about dreams and following them. If I had to guess, I would guess that she never meant to get stuck in that small town with a man like my father. She must not have known who he really was. But for some reason, one that I'll probably never know, she did, and I think she did it for me. I'm certain now that she must have thought it was a mistake well before she died.

This thought made me think again about the diary. I had forgotten for a moment that it was still under my mattress. I set Chance, who had finished nursing in his baby swing. I clipped his baby monitor to the waist of my jeans and then I grabbed the diary.

The last thing I wanted was to get caught with it by Lily. I wouldn't know how to explain myself to her as to why I had it. I didn't have permission and one lesson my father did teach me was that taking things without permission was stealing. The only thing about that with my father though, was that it wasn't really stealing if it was him stealing from me.

I check on Chance one more time to make sure he was situated good in his swing. I have the baby monitor on me, if he gets fussy, I'll just run right back up.

Reader was gone so this felt like the perfect opportunity to return the diary. I just needed to make it past Lily if she was somewhere in the house. Luckily, she wasn't. I could see her from my bedroom window out in the side garden picking flowers.

I headed down the stairs and then I entered Readers room. It's quite odd for the attic stairs to be on the first floor. I didn't question it before, but now that I'm at the bottom of them it's kind of weird. It's like they were added as an afterthought. But even so, why not put them in one of the upstairs bedrooms. It's odd because there are basically two flights of stairs instead of one. Which makes my chances of getting caught double.

The boxes where I got the diary were all the way towards the back. I headed back there, familiar with its location. I began to move the boxes that were in the way. Then I took the diary out from under my shirt where I had put it so if I had run into Lily, she wouldn't have seen it. I tucked it back in the box. I was about to close the tote back up when a photo I hadn't seen before caught my eye. It was a family photo of Lily, a man who must be her late husband Bill, and a side profile of their daughter Poppy. I flipped it over to see if there was a date. There was, August nineteen sixty-nine. What I was looking at confused me. If the photo hadn't of been old and the girl wasn't with Lily and her husband, I would have been sure it was a photo of me around seven years old.

I put the picture in my pocket. I closed the lid and ran as fast as I could downstairs then back upstairs. I dug through my things looking for a picture I had of me. When I found it, I held Poppy next to the one of me where I was the same exact age that I had gotten from my teacher that year. It was my side profile. I'm smiling at my science partner. We looked identical from the side. This Poppy, the girl with the same name... she has to be my momma and that's why my momma left me that address even though it's not the same exact address. It's the same town and same state, just a different house. Lily must have moved sometime after my momma left.

I take a deep breath. I think I might have finally figured it out.

26

Emily

Reader took forever to get back. I was dying to tell him what I found out... what I think I know. Who I think I am. The last thing I wanted to do was keep something else from him. I had learned the hard way that I didn't like him upset with me. So, getting this information off my chest was my top priority. Probably more so than his injuries. Truth be told, I almost forgot about them. Remembering only when he pulled in with a bandage on his right hand.

Chance had fallen asleep in his swing while I was in the attic. He was awake now and we were sitting on the front porch waiting for Reader to come home. I had the two pictures in my pocket ready to whip them out and show him the very first second that I could. I was both nervous and excited.

That was until he got out of his truck and I saw his face. His right eye was swollen almost completely shut now and when he got closer, I saw that he had gotten what looked to be four stitches in his forehead.

"Oh my God Reader!"

He walks past us.

"It's nothing. Don't worry about it."

He walked into the house leaving me and Chance on the porch. Not even acknowledging him.

I gave myself three minutes to feel the hurt I was feeling before I decided that was enough. I didn't deserve to be ignored or pushed aside. Furthermore, Chance didn't deserve to be ignored.

Feeling quite full of myself, I decided I was going to go back into the house and demand him to apologize to me.

Instead, I walked in and overheard a conversation between Reader and Lily. I was curious about what was being said so I stayed far enough back not to be seen but close enough to hear.

"I was just so angry Lily. I hadn't been that mad in a long time. I wasn't even this mad when I lost my brother or my parents. But to call him a retard. I lost my cool so quickly and I just went off."

Lily was shaking her head as he was talking. I could see a portion of her face. She looked at him with sadness and concern.

"He's an innocent child. Who says something like that? You have to be pretty heartless and cold to be able to pick on a helpless child."

Lily exhales.

"Unfortunately child, there's a lot of that out in the world. Believe me."

I believed her. Did Reader?

My father was one of those people. There were plenty of people back home like that, Alicia, and Tate even though Tate did show us some heart finally, and now those guys. I am afraid with Chance in our lives we are going to find out a lot more just how cold hearted and mean people can really be.

"If I get this mad now, when he's still a baby... how am I supposed to handle this when he gets older? I'll go crazy protecting him!"

Reader runs his fingers, the uninjured ones through his hair. I noticed that's his way of responding to frustration. He's got mannerisms that I can't help but find extremely attractive. Which reminds me about what we were supposed to do tonight. I don't think that's happening now, which disappoints me even more.

Chance was starting to squirm. I didn't want him to make any loud noises and give away our eavesdropping. So I took a few quiet steps back, turned and started to head towards the stairs. I didn't make it up two steps when I heard Reader say to Lily that he's going to ask me to marry him so that he can keep us all safe.

I walk as quietly as I can to my room and quietly shut the door. I put Chance back in his swing. I make a mental note to check if I am putting him in his swing too often. Then I am back to Readers words.

He wants to marry me to *keep us safe.*

Holy shit!

Holy shit!

Holy shit!

I don't know how I feel about that. Should I be more excited? Excited that this beautiful, caring man wants to marry me and make us an official family. Am I being a bit too lackluster in my response? Why am I not more excited?

He wants to marry me to keep us safe... shouldn't he be marrying me because he loves me? Does he love me? He's never said so. We've also never done anything that people in love do. We've done things friends would do. And yes, friends can fall in love even without intimacy. But something about that scares me that he just wants to marry me because it would be the right thing to do… for us all. I don't know if I can go along with that. I'm certain I want real love to be the reason. Not obligation or pity or even safety.

How do I turn him down if he does ask and if I do will that ruin everything for us? Will it ruin Chances shot at having a real father around? Do I say yes and sacrifice myself and my feelings for him? Is that what my momma did for me? If so, look at how that turned out. Not good. Not good at all.

We stayed in my room until dinner time. I was dreading going downstairs, but I was starving because of the light lunch and since sex was probably not happening tonight, I was more than ready for dinner.

Reader was already seated at the table. When he saw us he smiled. That was good news. Maybe his bad mood was over. I still deserve an apology though.

"I thought maybe you guys were asleep, I didn't want to wake you."

I set Chance in his baby seat that we keep for him in the kitchen.

"We weren't." I replied kindly. Trying not to sound off any alarms or show that I was upset and now worried about his intentions for us. I don't know if I succeeded.

"How was the rest of your guy's afternoon? Any issues?"

I shook my head no as I sat down in my seat that was now next to his, not across from him like usual.

He takes this opportunity to reach for my hand under the table and holds it tightly while I try and wrap this new seating arrangement around my mind.

He leans closer to me.

"I'm sorry I was such a jerk when I got home. I guess I hadn't quite simmered down yet. Are you upset with me? I would understand if you were."

I took a second to decide if I was still upset. A little... more hurt than anything.

"No, I'm not upset, (a half lie) although I don't think it was fair for you to practicality ignore us. But I accept your apology. Thank you."

"No, thank you Emily."

He pulls my hand out from under the table and kisses the top of it. Then he slides his chair out, gets up and picks Chance up hugging him tightly.

I heard him whisper, "*I'm so sorry little guy, daddy won't let that happen again.*"

That statement brought tears to my eyes because I know deep down what happened today won't be the last time, even if Reader and I have the best intentions of protecting him.

27

Reader

I felt bad. I shouldn't have treated Emily that way. She didn't deserve that, and I know she was just as upset as I was. I should have been there for her instead of sitting in my own rage. I was acting selfishly.

Not that it's any excuse but I was still hot. It hurt like hell in the emergency room. Doesn't matter how numb they think they got me, getting these stitches still hurt like a bitch. And the only thing that should have been the bitch was Chad. He better not say another word to me about anything, especially Chance, because I'll do the same thing I did to him earlier today but worse. And I'll make sure nobody else is around.

I saw him hobble into the emergency room after I did. It looked like he hurt his ankle too. He didn't know I was there. He looked like he was going to cry. And then I heard him scream out in pain as they were stitching him up. At least I was man enough to stomach that shit. He was definitely being a little bitch. That was enough for me to keep my mouth shut and not jump him at the hospital. That and

I figured making a scene wouldn't be the best thing for Chance. He needs me and so does Emily.

Which is why I decided that I am going to ask her to marry me. She did put my name on his birth certificate, but I wanted to be more. I want to be more. I want to be a real family. He's going to need a father and there will never come a day when he needs to know that I am not his real birth father and that his momma and me weren't always married.

It feels like the right thing to do. Hell, it feels like the only thing to do.

I can also keep Emily's secret for her. I can keep them both safe. I'm certain of it. Chance will grow up and never know the difference. Neither will anyone else.

Emily and I had plans for tonight, but I don't know if I will be able to follow through after the kind of day we had. It would be a great ending to the day, don't get me wrong. I've wanted to be with her since she first showed up. Since our first day in the library. I knew then that despite her being pregnant, that we had chemistry. I was attracted to her. But it wasn't just that. It was more. There was a bond as well. A bond that clearly involves Chance.

I know she heard me talking to Lily. Or at least I know she heard the part about me saying that I wanted to marry her. I also saw her tiptoe up the stairs. She wouldn't do that unless she didn't want me to know she was there. So approaching her tonight, I'm not sure how I should. Do I ask her to marry me first or do I make love to her despite this horrible day and then ask her after?

What if she says no? If I ask her before we make love, then there will be no love making. If I ask her after we make love and she says no, then it will ruin the *just made love* moment. I am torn about what the right thing to do is.

Maybe I should start by telling her that I know she was eavesdropping on my and Lily's conversation and go from there. Or maybe calling her out on it would embarrass her. Maybe I don't say a thing. I don't want to embarrass her. I feel like I'm staring at a brick wall, and I don't know if I should go left or right. Maybe I just ask her later when it's a special moment. Just for her. A romantic moment. She deserves that.

What I do know is that I loved today up until the time Chad showed his big ugly face. Then he ruined the rest of it.

I also know that if he ever tries to do something like that again, he won't ruin my day... but I'll ruin the rest of his life. I'm not messing around when it comes to my son or Emily.

28

Emily

I didn't know if Reader was going to come to my room tonight. I expected him to check on us like he always does but I wasn't sure what else would transpire after that.

I still had the pictures to show him but hearing him say he was going to ask me to marry him feels like it threw everything else off. Nothing seemed as important and everything else seemed awkward at the same time. It's a weird feeling.

All I wanted was for things to feel normal in my life. I know that is asking a lot especially with my situation with Chance and being here in this house, but that didn't mean I... we couldn't find some sort of normal for us. Drama free, trauma free, stress free. I... we deserve that.

Was that actually a possibility for us? I had no clue.

I had been so wrapped up in all the details of the day, the fight with Chad, discovering the picture, Reader wanting to marry me, that I hadn't really thought too much about what Poppy being my momma really means, if she is actually my momma.

As awkward as dinner was for me, I tried to act as normally as possible. But realizing at that moment that Lily could be my grandmother had me spiraling a bit. I wanted to burst out and tell her... tell them, but I was also terrified to say anything at all. I mean how do I really know for sure? This whole similarity between us, this address... it wasn't the same but close, and Poppy having the same name could just be one huge, giant, sick and twisted coincidence.

It could not be true, and I was almost willing to just blurt it all out in the open without even really knowing for sure. That's why I wanted to run it by Reader first. To make sure I actually made some sense. If I convinced Lily I was her dead granddaughter and then it turns out I wasn't, that could break her heart all over again. Or worse, give her a stroke or something worse than that. I've seen what news like this does to people in the movies. I'd die if Lily suffered because of it. I can't be that reason. I wouldn't be able to live with myself.

I heard Reader's soft knock on my door. He always knocks softly in case Chance was sleeping.

"Come in." I said loud enough for him to hear me.

Chance was awake and will be until his bedtime in about an hour and a half. He's always awake this time of night. I feel like now is his most active time and it has become my second favorite time with him.

Reader sees Chance lying on my bed next to me and walks over to him and scoops him up then sits. He has this voice he uses when he talks to him that is so sweet. It's not baby-like but it's softer than his normal voice. Chance responds back to him with coos. He is also trying to mimic Readers' lips. I don't think I've seen anything that makes me happier than when I see them like this together.

"He's growing so fast, I can hardly believe it."

Reader looks over at me and smiles. I don't respond. Mostly because I don't feel the need too. My face says enough.

He kisses Chances cheeks and then sets him back down on the bed between us.

"Em..."

Before he finishes, I have something to say.

"Wait, I need to tell you something first."

My consciousness was getting to me. I needed to tell him that I overheard him.

I stayed quiet for a few seconds and before I lost my nerve...

"Two things actually."

Reader gives me a concerned look, so I put his mind at ease.

"It's nothing bad. Just something I may have figured out today. But I wanted to start by telling you that I... that I heard what you said to Lily when you came home from the hospital today. I heard everything you said. I was listening and I'm sorry."

The next thirty seconds were terrifying.

He reaches over Chance and grabs both of my hands and holds them in his.

"It's alright Em."

"I don't really feel good about it."

"About what? Which part?"

I take a deep breath.

"All of it."

He adjusts his legs to get closer to me. He still has my hands in his.

"Can you explain please?"

I thought about what I wanted to say before I said it. I wanted to tell him about the pictures first, but I know that part needs to wait until after we talk about us. I wanted to know where he stood on his feelings for me before I dropped that huge bomb on him. It was more important to me.

I take a deep breath.

"Okay... so... I did realize what it would mean when I put you as the father on his birth certificate. I knew that it would make you responsible for him and his care. And because you wanted that, of course I wanted that too. I want that. I do. But today, I don't know... it was hard, that was hard. It puts everything into perspective. I think about what the future could possibly look like for him. For me... for us if you do choose to stay with us. It'll be hard..."

He squeezes my hands interrupting me.

"Em, I'm not going anywhere. I want you to know that. I'll choose you two every day. I promise."

I look away for a moment. I don't want him to look me in the eyes because what I want to say next, I am ashamed to feel.

"See that's just the thing. I kind of want to make sure you're choosing me."

I pause and wait to see how he replies.

"Can you explain more please."

"Sure. I mean I don't want you to want to marry me just because Chance needs a father and needs protection. I want you to marry me because you're in love with me. Is that wrong of me to want?"

I exhale.

"Great, I feel completely selfish now."

I pull my hands out of his.

"Em..."

I continue to look down, which causes the tears that escaped my eyes to drop into my lap. Reader reaches up to softly wipe what's left of them away. I let him, then I lean my face into his hand.

"Come here."

He pulls at my right arm with his free hand to get me to come closer to him. I resist at first and then I don't. I want this. I want to be in his arms. I want to be consoled.

I allow him to pull me into his arms. I lay my head on his chest as he holds me tight.

"I can assure you Emily, with every bone in my body that I am not wanting to marry you just because of Chance. I'd be lying if I didn't say he was half the reason but regardless I am very, very much in love with you... both of you. I want us to be a family."

I looked up at him stunned.

"You're in love with me?"

He smiles and my belly flops.

"I am. Have been for a while now."

"You have?"

"Yes."

He laughs about something. I'm not sure what. I don't really care what. The next thing I feel is his lips on top of mine.

He kissed me for five minutes straight I swear to God. And the only reason I think he stopped was because Chance started to cry.

He pulls back and looks down at Chance who's still lying between us.

"Is he hungry?" he asks me.

I look over at the clock on my nightstand.

"Yeah, it's definitely time for him to eat."

Reader leans down and kisses Chance on the top of his little head then stands up.

"I'll let you feed him and get him to bed. Is it okay if I come back in an hour?"

His question caught me by surprise.

"You want to come back?"

"I do."

"Oh! Are we going to... you know..."

Reader laughs and I turn bright red, embarrassed that I even asked.

"We can. If you want too. Or we can wait. I just want to be near you. Is that okay?"

I nodded. Still terrified out of my mind.

"Yeah, that's okay."

He plants a quick kiss on my lips and walks out of the room. Shutting the door behind him.

I didn't have much time to digest the conversation or what was going to possibly happen later because Chance was now fully upset that he is not eating and he was fully letting me know.

I never did get to part two of the conversation.

<h1 style="text-align:center">29</h1>

Reader

I waited a full hour to go back, but if I'm being honest it felt like three. I was nervous. I know she didn't see that side of me an hour earlier, but I was freaking out.

I'm not expecting her to make love to me tonight. I would never force her to do anything she wasn't ready for. But I meant it when I said I loved her. I meant it when I said that I had been in love with her for a while.

Getting over the fact that she didn't trust me enough to tell me about her situation with Tate, Alicia, and her father was hard. It hurt. But I realized that life is way too short to hang onto pain like that. She's going through something that's extremely hard, harder than the hurt I feel, and she was doing it alone.

I know what that feels like myself. Lily was here for me, and I am more than grateful for that, but it's still not the same as having someone your age that you love to talk to and share your deep, dark feelings with.

I was angry when my parents died, but I was even angrier now that my baby brother was taken away from us. I guess I had never fully grieved. Partly because I was younger and couldn't fully grasp death and at that time, I still had my parents. But when my parents died... it felt like I lost all three of them at the same time. I had to grieve them all at the same time. Part of grief is anger, and I had to keep that in because I couldn't show it around Lily. That would just be unfair and hard for her. She's been my only support since they were taken from me, and she was also still suffering from her own losses.

I had no place to put that anger until I started writing it into poems. Poems I'd never share with anyone. Ever. They were dark and they wouldn't make anyone happy. People want to be surrounded by happy things. Not sadness. So, I hid them in a safe place. I don't know if I'll ever show them to anyone, not even Emily.

Emily's been through a lot and the more I thought about her situation, and when I held Chance close... I get it. I totally do. She couldn't take the chance and have him end up someplace other than with her or worse, dead like they wanted. I chose to put myself in her shoes and understand that it wasn't about me. It wasn't even about her. It was about Chance.

I knocked on her door softly and listened for her to tell me to come in. But there was nothing, so I slowly opened it. Emily was asleep with Chance still in her bed. She had fallen asleep nursing him. I had seen her nurse before, plenty of times, but she had always been semi-private about it aside from when she was in labor and starting to nurse. She was good at keeping covered. This was the first time I've seen her breast completely exposed, her not shying away from me. Chance was not latched on but had fallen asleep too, tucked into the crook of her elbow.

I don't think she could look more beautiful. I took a moment to take her in. She looked at peace asleep. A few strands of her light brown hair have fallen over her face. Just enough to cover one eye but not completely. I could see her chest rising and falling with every breath she took. And her breast... full and soft at the same time, with light, almost pure white skin. Her dark brown nipple was still at a point from nursing Chance. This image of her, one that will forever be burned into my mind, just made me want her more. Not in a ravishing way, but in a tender way. In a very slow, kiss every inch of her body softly way.

I knew I was probably going to startle her and definitely embarrass her when I picked Chance up to lay him in his crib for the night. The little guy had been doing so well and only getting up once a night to nurse the last couple of nights. To my calculations, we had at least four to five hours before he was due to wake up again.

"Oh my God, I'm so sorry." she whispered as she scrambled to tuck her breast back into her shirt.

I laid Chance down in his bed and turned back to her.

"For what?" I whispered back.

She wipes her eyes and then starts to comb through her hair.

"I fell asleep. I didn't mean to."

I chuckled quietly.

"Emily it's fine. You're tired. Being a mom is exhausting."

"Yeah, you can say that again!"

"Being a mom is exhausting." I repeated but as a joke.

It worked because she smiled.

"Do you mind if I use the bathroom?"

"Of course not. I'll be here when you get back. I'll just watch Chance sleep."

I said that as a joke also, kind of. I honestly could just watch him sleep. Emily smiled and left the room.

When she returned things were the most awkward they have ever been.

"Do you want me to leave?" I asked unsure if she wanted to go back to sleep.

"Oh no, you don't have to... unless you want to. Do you want to?"

"No."

She took a deep breath.

"Okay."

"Do you want to lay down? I can just spend the night?"

It seemed like she had to think about it.

"Sure."

We both climbed into bed and covered up. She's facing me and I'm now looking into her eyes. This is the closest we've ever been, physically and emotionally. I smile and tuck the same loose strand of hair from moments ago behind her ear. She's so beautiful. All I wanted to do was kiss her.

"Reader." she says, then pauses.

I leaned in slowly.

"There's something I wanted to tell you."

But she's too late, my lips are already on hers, kissing her. Deeply this time. Passionately.

I pull back for one second.

"I saw your breast."

"I know."

We kissed again. I pull back.

"It was beautiful. I'm kind of jealous of Chance." I laughed, but leaned back in to kiss her, not needing a response. Just needing her lips.

"Do you want to do this Em?"

"What, kiss you?"

"Well yes, but also make love?"

"Oh... yes, I do."

"Okay."

I stop kissing her and roll out of bed to pull all my clothes off. Emily is watching me. I see her eyes widening when I take off my boxers. I'm standing in front of her completely naked, my body already responding fully to the intimate moment. Her response makes me smile.

I climb back into bed and help her take off her pajamas that she had put on after I had left her room earlier. Now I'm not the only one who is naked. And I was wrong earlier, she's more beautiful now. This is the most beautiful I've ever seen her. Actually, she's the most beautiful woman I've ever seen.

I kiss her again. This time with me lightly perched on top of her. Her body felt amazing under mine. It was soft and smooth. I caressed her right breast first and then her left.

"Are they tender?" I asked.

"A little, but I don't mind. Maybe don't squeeze them too hard or you know... suck."

I chuckled.

"Chance would be so mad if I drink his milk."

Emily laughs.

"Yes, he would."

She pauses then asks, "But would you really?"

"Really what?"

I didn't know what she meant, I was too busy still kissing them to comprehend her question, making sure I gave them both enough attention because selfishly I wanted to.

"Would you really drink my milk?"

"Oh, umm... no not drink it. But if I got a little taste I would not be upset."

I looked up at her.

"Is that gross?"

"No." was all she said.

I was relieved to hear that. I didn't want her to think she was gross or that her milk was gross. What she is doing for Chance is such a big deal. Such a huge advantage for him and his health and she's doing it selfishly. Treating him like he is in fact *her own.*

"I want to make love to you now. Is that okay?"

"Mmmhmmm."

I sprung up and grabbed the condom that I had in the pocket of my jeans. I opened it up and pulled it on. Emily watching the whole time waiting for me. Waiting for me to make love to her.

And we did, for two hours. Until we were both too tired to move. When we were finished, I held her close to me with her head on my chest until we were both almost asleep.

"Emily?"

"Yeah."

"Did you want to tell me something?"

Emily doesn't move.

"No, it can wait until the morning."

"Are you sure?"

"Yep."

"Okay... Em?

"Hmmm?"

"I love you."

"I love you Reader."

I kissed her twice on the top of her head and fell asleep with her words still ringing in my ears. The best four words I've ever heard all at once.

Chance Worth Taking

We slept peacefully all night. Chance didn't even wake up for his middle of the night feeding. It was an amazing night of firsts.

30

Emily

I woke up that next morning alone. Reader was not in my bed, but he had left a note.

I forgot I had to go pick up some furniture that Lily had made and needed to leave early because it is a six-hour round trip. I hope you and Chance have a wonderful day. And his first time sleeping all night!? What a big boy! I'll see you later. I love you, Reader.

I'm not going to lie; I was a bit bummed he wasn't here. Last night felt so... ummm... magical. It was wonderful. He's a great kisser and a great love maker. He kept telling me how beautiful I was, which felt really good to hear. Nobody's told me that before. And right now, I feel like my body belongs to the baby. It has for over a year now. Reader made me feel like it was my own last night. And a part of me... well all of me, was thrilled he enjoyed it thoroughly.

I had never experienced that kind of love making before. The few boys I had spent any time with didn't make me feel like he did last night. He made me feel cared for and he made me a priority. With the others, it had always just been about them. Reader was different. He made me feel special. He was also the first to say he loved me. He's the first I've loved back.

But I still didn't get a chance to talk to him about the diary and the pictures I found in the attic.

Chance started to stir in his bed. I could hear him on the verge of tears, so I hopped out of bed to grab him before he really started to cry.

He was so cute lying there with his sleepy eyes.

"Hi beautiful boy! You slept all night, didn't you? You're such a good boy! I bet you are starving!?"

His reply was to scream his little head off. Apparently, he wasn't in the mood for praise.

I fed Chance and took him downstairs to look for Lily. If she wasn't busy, I was going to see if she could watch Chance while I showered and got ready for the day. She had been watching him for me in the mornings when she wasn't busy. Otherwise, I had to take him into the bathroom with me, which was fine too.

I found her in the kitchen drinking coffee and reading the newspaper.

"Good morning, Lily."

She looked up and smiled.

"Good morning Emily, and Chance too."

She rose from her chair to take Chance into her arms. She started talking in baby talk and kissing his cheeks that have become extra chunky lately.

"I was going to grab a shower if that's okay?"

"Sure! I'd be happy to spend some time with him. Take your time."

I leaned in to kiss him on the head and then I headed back upstairs.

"Thank you!" I called back.

If she ends up being my grandmother, then that will mean that Chance is her great grandson... *kind of.* I wonder if she will think of him as her great grandson. I feel like she would, but I can't be for certain. She treats him so good now, I can't think of her being any different honestly. Maybe she will never know the truth about him. Maybe she doesn't need to know.

My shower felt amazing, but I could only think about Reader. I was really missing him. Of all the days he had to leave for most of the day, it had to be this day. The one after we finally make love. I was dying to see him, and I was really hoping this day didn't drag on like some other days do.

Downstairs Lily had Chance outside, walking him around the trees. She was showing him the stream. I could see his little eyes widen as he looked up at their tall vastness. He is going to love it here when he is old enough to really enjoy it. I can picture us running around outback and through the whole garden. Playing hide and seek around the trees, splashing in the stream, eating lunch on a big blanket, maybe even reading him poetry. I could see it all now. I couldn't be any happier than I am at this moment now. I feel like I finally got what I truly deserved in life.

31

Lily

I pulled the pump of my shotgun back and heard it cock. The sound is loud in my right ear. I always keep one hidden near the front entry. This is the first time I've ever had to use it.

His face is familiar, and it takes me a minute to recognize it. But I do. It's the same face that took my daughter and my granddaughter away from me. A face I hate so much I feel it deep in my gut. It is taking everything in my body to not shoot him right in that face that I hate so much.

"Emily go on now, get behind me." I say not moving the end of the barrel an inch.

Jack must have grabbed her when she answered the doorbell. Luckily, I was on my way to answer it is well, or he might have taken them without me knowing.

Emily can't move. Jack had pulled out a knife and put it to her throat. Chance is asleep in her arms.

"I don't want no trouble here Lily. I just came looking for what's rightfully mine."

"There aint nothin' here that belongs to you Jack. You took them away eighteen years ago. There ain't nothing left. You took everything I had."

"I think you must be mistaken Lily."

"Noooo..., I'm not mistaken. You took my family away from me and then they died! What's to mistake? If poppy had stayed here with me, that would have never happened! Now get the hell out of my house! There's nothing left here for you to take. You've taken everything you could."

Jack looks away from me to whisper something in Emily's ear. Tears start to trail down her cheeks. But she stays silent aside from the muffled sobs she is trying her hardest not to let out, probably trying not to wake up Chance.

"Why don't you just let her go. She's holding a baby. Have you no soul?"

Jack laughs.

"That's rich. Weren't you the one ready to throw your pregnant daughter out onto the street?"

Emily's eyes widened.

"You don't know what you are talking about."

"Oh, I think I do." he smirks, sure of himself.

"You were ready to cast out your own daughter and granddaughter. I'm the one who had to come in and save them. Give them a home."

"That's not true. I was hurt but I accepted it. She was better off here. I don't know what you did to convince her otherwise, but it worked and now she is gone!" I yelled back forgetting that Chance is sleeping. I can feel my blood starting to boil up to my face.

He laughs.

"I'm not doing this with you. I'm getting what I came for and were going. Where is it?" he asks Emily.

He starts to push Emily forward even though I still have my shotgun pointed at him.

"Tell me!" he yells. Chance startles in his sleep.

"Why would she go with you?" I asked to keep him from moving any further.

He looks back at me and smiles.

My confusion thickens. Things don't make any sense.

"Emily, do you know him?" I ask confused.

She swallows a sob down.

"Father why are you here?" she whispers.

Her words were quiet, but I heard her loud and clear.

Father? It can't be?

"Jack is your father?"

I feel the emotions of the possibilities rising in my throat. I feel sick. I looked between the two of them. Emily starts to cry harder. The tears are running down in two streams now.

Jack laughs loudly. Chance stirs again. Emily holds him tighter, but she can't move her head to look at him.

"He's okay." I tell her to ease her mind.

"I'm here because she took something that belongs to me, and I want it back."

The worst imaginable thought hits my mind.

"No!"

I shake my head in disbelief hoping my thoughts are wrong.

"The baby?" I whispered not wanting to say what I just said.

Jack realizes what I'm asking. He let out a scoff. His eyes narrowing, as if he was offended. I watch his teeth bare though his twisted smirk.

"You think I'm the father? That's rich."

He lets out a dry laugh, then sneers, his eyes darkening.

"I don't think I'm the messed up one here Lily. I took care of my daughter. Provided for her. I was going to continue to care for her. Before she took off, clearly not knowing what was best for her."

I stand there silently. Not sure what to do next but to make sure he doesn't move.

"Where is it, Emily?" he asks her again, lowering his face closer to hers as he pushes the knife further into her neck but not drawing blood yet.

"You took my money when you left, and I know he gave you money for keeping the baby when he came here to see you. You stole from me, so I'm not leaving here without it or I'm not leaving here without you and that baby. It's your choice. I'll get my money one way or another!"

"Her name is Meadow!" I yelled.

Emily looks at me confused. Her eyes widening in question.

"What?" Jack asked.

"She named her Meadow; Poppy named her Meadow not Emily. She hated the name Emily. She's not Emily!"

Jack laughs, shaking his head clearly entertained.

"Wow, this a great! So, she's been living right under your nose this whole time and you didn't even know?"

I didn't. You made me believe she was dead.

"How would I know Jack? You took them from me and then you told me they died! You mailed me the ashes!"

Meadow starts sobbing loudly and it wakes up Chance. His eyes open slowly, taking in his surroundings. His little lip pushes out getting ready to cry.

I stare at Emily and Chance fully knowing my emotions are getting harder to control but also trying to keep myself calm. Is Emily my granddaughter? Is Emily Meadow? How can that be? How could I not have known? She's been here for months."

"Is the baby yours?" I ask just to confirm.

He laughs again.

"You've got to be kidding me! Hell no, that kid ain't mine. But the money is, and I want it back!"

"We don't know nothing about no money so I'm afraid you have wasted a trip, Jack. Get out of my house!"

Chance is now crying. I can see Jack getting uncomfortable.

"Shut that kid up now!" he demands. Squeezing Meadow closer to him.

"He needs to eat, he's hungry." her words cracking in fear.

"Then we're going now. You can feed him in the car. Right after we go get the money. Where is it?" he demands.

Meadow doesn't answer, her cries now match Chances.

This isn't happening. I won't lose my family to him again.

I tightened the barrel of the gun back up to my face and into my sights. I see Reader creeping up behind them with a shovel in his hand. I know I need to keep Jack distracted so he doesn't hear him coming up the porch stairs.

"I may not have known she was my granddaughter, but I will protect her and my great grandchild from you if it means my life. You have until the count of ten to get the hell out of here and stay out."

Jack looks very angry now.

"You aren't the one in charge here old lady. You shoot me, I'll slit her throat before you do. Then you will lose your granddaughter forever and for real this time."

I pointed the shot gun to the ceiling and fire. Jack flinches just enough so that Reader is able to hit him in the head with a shovel. His arm drops with the knife still in it and Emily free's herself from his grip. Jack falls to the floor holding his head with his free hand. The knife is still in his other hand, gripped tightly. He stands back up searching for who hit him. Reader brings the shovel back up in the air ready to swing at him again. Jack lunges for Meadow and Chance who are heading for the back door. I pump the gun one more time and fire. Jack drops slowly to the ground. His eyes locked on me as he realizes what I have done. I hear his breath start to labor. He's bleeding out quickly from the hole in his chest.

"You took my daughter and granddaughter from me. Broke my heart for years. Now I broke yours, you bastard!"

Jack lay there bleeding out while his cold dying eyes were locked on mine.

"I should have done that a long time ago." I whispered just before he took his final breath. I watched him pass over.

You'll never take another thing from me again.

32

Emily

Lily walks over to me and wraps me into a hug. I hugged her back.

"I didn't know Meadow." she whispers.

"I'm so sorry, I didn't know." she repeats.

"I didn't know either until just a few days ago."

She pulls me back.

"How did you get here? How did you find this place?"

"Oh."

I pulled out my momma's locket from under my t-shirt. I opened it up and showed her the little piece of paper that was inside.

Lily takes it and unfolds it.

"She left this for you?"

"She did."

"Well, isn't that somethin'."

She hugged me again as tightly as she could while I still held Chance in my arms. My head is on her chest, her hand holding it to keep me close. I felt loved and safe. It's what I always dreamed about. What I dreamed family felt like.

"That's our old house. Hmm... it's gone now, burnt to the ground about twelve years ago. Yet you still ended up here? It's a living miracle!"

She kisses the top of my head.

I realized then that I never had the chance to check the address out. Maybe I would have known Lily was my grandmother sooner, or maybe not. I guess I got caught up in Reader and this place that I forgot. I can't be sure what the reasons were. Here felt like home. That's all I knew. Maybe I was afraid I'd have to leave if I discovered my family was at that address. Maybe they weren't good people. Maybe I was afraid to find out. Maybe I felt deep down that I wanted to belong here instead. With Reader and Lily.

Lucky for us we didn't have to choose.

"Oh, how I've missed you. All these years..."

I've missed you too...

It didn't matter that we never met before. It still felt true.

"I'm going to call this in." Reader says from behind us.

Lily and I pull apart, snapping back to reality.

My father is lying on the floor dead in a pool of his own blood. The knife still sits in his hand, his grip released.

Lily finally realizing what she had done, looks at me.

"I'm so sorry Meadow."

She has a lot of fright in her eyes.

I know she's apologizing to me because she killed my father.

I shake my head, tears forming again in my eyes.

"I'm glad." I whisper.

It takes a bit, but she smiles and then excuses herself leaving Reader, Chance, and myself there with my father's body.

Reader takes me in his arms.

"You two should go upstairs. This is going to take a while. I know he's hungry and scared. I don't think you should stay down here. Unless you really want too?"

I shake my head no.

"I don't want to be around him any more than I have too."

"Okay. Good. I'll come get you when I need you. I'm sure they will want a statement."

I had Chance settled down, but he was starting to cry again.

"I'll go feed him. Reader…"

He's still holding me.

"Yeah?"

"Thank you."

"You're welcome, Emily."

"Actually, it's Meadow."

He pulls back.

"What?"

I laugh. It's not funny but my emotions are all mixed up.

"Yeah, apparently my name is Meadow." I shrug.

He pulls me back into a hug, squeezes me tight then let's go.

"Good Lord. You can fill me in later."

I smile and head up the stairs to finally feed Chance.

Thirty minutes later Lily knocks on my door.

"Can I come in?" she asks.

"Of course!"

She comes in and sits next to me on the bed. I'm still holding Chance. There isn't any part of me that wants to put him down. Not for a while at least. Today was the scariest day of my life. And I've had a few.

"I want to start by apologizing."

"It's okay Lily, really, you've already said enough downstairs. I didn't know either."

She takes my hand and holds it in hers. Then pauses.

"I know. But I should have recognized you. I see it now. I see Poppy."

"Oh…"

Her words hit my chest like a thousand bricks.

"It's not your fault." I whispered.

Now I'm trying not to cry again. I've cried enough for the rest of my life.

I felt a tear let loose from my left eye first and then my right. I did all I could to stop them.

"Just the same… I should have. You're my own flesh and blood."

I didn't want her to feel guilt. She didn't deserve that. She was lied to. She didn't have any way to know the truth. Neither of us did. I know how my father is, who he was.

"I didn't even know about you, I mean… I remember my momma talking about you but all of that was before the age of four. My father told me that all of my family was dead. He even had obituaries to show me. One of you and one of my momma's father. Your pictures were different though; they weren't your faces. They were someone else's. So, I never thought for once that tiny piece of paper would lead me to you. I don't know what I was thinking about why it was in her locket. I just knew it was someplace I should go. I thought that maybe she lived here once, and I'd at least feel her presence. I didn't think about my father knowing where to find me. I didn't think about family. I guess I didn't think about much."

She sighs.

"You father was always a piece of work. He came from a bad family. Lots of abuse. I could never figure out what Poppy saw in him."

It was strange to hear her name said out loud. I haven't heard it since I was four.

"I think she found herself pregnant and she was trying to do the right thing by you. She clearly didn't know who your father really was. I wish she hadn't left. I wish she would have stayed here."

"Me too."

"You said you knew a couple of days ago?"

"Oh yes, hold on."

I stood up and set Chance in his swing. This was a good enough reason to put him down.

I walked over to my nightstand and pulled out the two pictures I had kept. The two I was going to show Reader. I handed them to her.

"This was in the attic when Reader and I went up there for the swaddling blanket." I said pointing to the one in her left hand.

"And this one I had. One of my teachers had taken it and had given it to me. We are almost identical, and we have to be close to the same age. This one has her name on the back. The same name as my momma."

Lily starts to cry.

"Oh, dear sweet Lord... heavens. What a miracle this is. A heavenly miracle."

She's staring at the photos in disbelief. The fact that she thought we were dead, both of us, my heart is breaking for her at this moment. I've had a few days to adjust to knowing she was possibly my grandmother. She's had about an hour. And the most stressful hour ever.

"I think momma was watching over me. She told me before she died that I might need to leave. She tucked a suitcase in my closet and told me not to forget about it."

I got up and pulled out the suitcase from my closet. Lily looks over to it and her eyes widen.

"That's Poppy's. She took it when she left. I can't believe I'm just seeing that now. Heavens it's been here this whole time with you?"

I shake my head yes. I feel bad for her. I feel bad for me. We were so close to discovering each other this whole time. If she had opened the door that first night, we would have known then and saved all this time.

"She had hidden it and told me that *when* I needed to leave to remember it. This locket was in the pocket."

I pulled the locket out of my shirt again. Her eyes soften.

"I gave her that locket for her sixteenth birthday. She was so excited about it, she jumped up and down I swear for like twenty minutes. She hugged me like ten times."

That story brought a smile to my face but made me sad at the same time. Not sad for me... sad for Lily. I couldn't image what it would be like to lose your daughter in that way... to a man like my father and then be told we were both dead, having their ashes show up at your door and no other information.

"Um... those urns... those are fake." I said but with hesitation. I figured she knew the one was but maybe she didn't know they both were. She shakes her head, like she understands.

"My father took me to my momma's funeral. He wanted to make sure I saw her dead body, buried. He told me to *"remember this moment. That was what happened to people who didn't obey their husbands."* Which confused me because she died when he was at work. I was only four but it's an image that's permanently burned into my memory. I know where she is if you ever want to make the trip. He did bury her properly. I started visiting her when I was old enough to go out on my own."

"How did she die?"

"My father told me she overdosed. But I don't think she did any drugs. She had a couple friends that knew her, and I ran into one of them at the store when I was thirteen. She must have recognized me and approached me. She asked me how I was, asked if I was okay. I told her I was fine and then she told me to be careful, that she never had known my mom to do any drugs and that she loved me very much."

"Do you think it was your father?"

I nodded.

"I think so. There was a lot of fighting. I remember being scared. She always told me to go into my room and hide when he started yelling and hitting. So that's what I did. He drank a lot on weekends and some weeknights too. But when he was at work during the week, it was just her and I and we did so many fun things. Lots of pretending. I vaguely remember her telling me we were going on this big adventure. I think she was planning on leaving with me and maybe he found out or maybe he was tired of her defying him if that's what she was doing. I woke up one morning and she was sleeping on the couch. Or so I thought. My father was at work. I had to sit there with her the entire day wondering why she wouldn't wake up."

My head was down while I was telling this story. It was hard to say all that, and I just wanted to concentrate on getting it all out. Lily was the only one I've ever told this too. I was nervous and I knew if I was looking at Lily I would probably cry. So, when I looked up, I didn't expect to see her sobbing.

"I'm sorry." I whispered. Desperately trying to hold my tears back, which was now impossible to do.

Maybe now wasn't a good time to tell her all this.

"It's not your fault dear; you have nothing to be sorry for."

"There's one other thing."

Lily looks at me with concern.

"It's nothing bad. But when Reader and I were in the attic looking for baby stuff, I found a diary in one of the boxes up there. Actually, it fell out of one when the box tipped over. I took it so I could read it. It was my momma's from when she was pregnant with me."

"Oh Meadow, what a gift!"

I smiled.

"I thought so too. I didn't know it was about me for sure when I read it, but now I know that it was.

Lily leaned in and hugged me. I could get so used to these hugs.

"It's back up in the attic, I can show you where if you ever want to read it. If you haven't already."

"I haven't. Thank you, Meadow, for everything. For coming here. For bringing us together. For staying. I could never tell you how much this means to me to have you here now. It's... it's just... everything."

"I have a few more pictures of momma and me, if you'd like to see them?"

"Oh, sweet dear, I would love that."

I pulled out the rest of the pictures I had and handed them to Lily for her to look at.

"There's a hair clip too. The clip part is broken but the flower is still intact."

I handed that to her next.

"A Poppy for Poppy. Her father gave this to her when she was five. It was her most favorite thing. She wore it all the time."

There was another tap on the door.

"Hey."

Reader heads over to Chance and picks him up, blowing raspberries into his neck. Chance loves it and laughs.

We are all looking at each other stunned.

"His first laugh! Oh, my goodness! Did he really just laugh?"

Reader blows another and Chance laughs again.

I could listen to that for hours.

Lily stands up and gives Chance and Reader a big hug.

"I'm so happy!"

She kisses Chance on his cheek.

"Do they need me downstairs?"

"They do."

"Alright. Let's get this over with."

Lily leaves the room and now it's just the three of us. I am still smiling from Chances first laugh and having us all here to witness it.

As a real family...

33

Reader

I've experienced a lot of death in my lifetime. Too much for my age. My mom, my dad, and my brother, which was hard, and it hurt so much. But what happened with Meadows' father that day was by far the scariest and craziest thing I had ever experienced firsthand.

Coming home from my trip and seeing an unknown truck in my driveway with a West Virginia license plate, I didn't have a good feeling about it. We get guests from time to time from out of town, but the look of this truck made me uncomfortable. That and I knew we weren't scheduled to receive any guests that day. Luckily, they didn't hear me pull in.

I heard the yelling right away. Then I heard Chance cry. I quietly grabbed the shovel I had left sitting on the corner of the house yesterday and very carefully crept towards the house. As I got closer to the door, I saw an unknown man's back and what looked like Emily held against him. The front door still wide open.

As I had carefully made it up two of the four steps, I saw Lily a few feet back holding a shotgun up to her face, pointed at the man. She didn't show any sign that she saw me, but I knew when she did. She pulled the gun in closer to her cheek and started yelling loudly. Then she shot it into the ceiling, which gave me the opportunity to hit him in the head with the shovel, knocking him off his guard.

All I could do was pray that Emily or Chance didn't get hurt. I trusted Lily. She was a tough lady. I figured the man was probably armed. It seemed like a standoff situation. I thought maybe he had a gun. I didn't know it was a knife until he hit the floor. I had to take my chances.

I didn't know it was her father until after he lunged at Emily again and Lily shot him. I put the two together pretty quickly. I didn't know that Emily was Lily's granddaughter.

I didn't know Emily was Meadow. I swear you can't even make this stuff up. This is the kind of thing you read in books. This is the kind of thing my mother would write, and it would become a best seller.

But no, it actually happened in real life. My life. Lily's life. Emily... I mean Meadow's life. Chance's life, even though he will never remember it.

She prefers Meadow now. Sometimes I still slip up and she just smiles at me awkwardly until I realize what I had said. Sometimes it takes me a while to realize. She doesn't take offense or get upset with me even though it's been three years. We've turned it into a joke so that it doesn't have to be a heavy memory, but there will come a day when I don't call her Emily anymore and it will become just a distant memory.

She's still herself, but she's better. She's family. We're a family.

"Come on buddy, we don't want to be late. Let's get your glasses on."

Chance looks up at me with his tiny little face.

"But I don't like 'em. They feel funny."

I feel for him.

"I know they do. But if you keep wearing them, then you will get used to them, and they will make you see better. Don't you want to see better?"

He folds his arms across his chest and makes a grumpy face.

"I see fine."

I can't help but laugh.

Which makes him laugh. It always does. Luckily he's not a bad kid. He just pretends to be sometimes. It never goes farther than a grumpy demeanor and it quickly changes the second I start laughing.

I tussle his hair and he squirms away from me. He really likes his hair to be combed neat. He starts patting it back down.

"If you don't put them on then we can't go to your soccer game that starts in a half hour and then if we don't go to that, then we can't go to the beach after like we planned. We were going to stay the night in that hotel with a pool, but I guess we don't need to go. I'll go tell momma you don't want to go. Be right back."

I head for the stairs but before I hit the second step he yells.

"Stop! Fine! I will wear them."

I turned around smiling at him. He smiles back. We put the glasses on.

"Momma!"

Meadow is making her way down the stairs. I already have our bags packed for the beach, all she had to do was get dressed.

"I feel like a whale."

Chance Worth Taking

I've heard that before.

I smile at the memory. Chance laughs.

"Momma's a whale!"

"Gee thanks!"

I lean in to kiss her on the lips.

"I think you need to watch what you say about yourself around him." I whisper.

"Yuck!" Chance says from behind us.

"Yucky kissy."

I turned around.

"Yucky huh?"

I grabbed him and threw him in the air. Then I kissed him all over his face. He squeals.

"Stop daddy, stop, yuck!"

Lily comes out of the kitchen with a couple of bottles of water for us and Chances special water bottle. The one he loves most and has to have at all times.

"There, all clean." she says and hands it to him.

He hugs her and tells her thanks.

"Okay we better get going."

"We're going to the beach Nana!"

Lily matches his enthusiasm.

"I heard. How fun!"

Then she looks at me and Meadow clearly concerned.

"Do you think it's a good idea to go now? What if the baby comes while your away?"

I lean in and kiss her on the cheek.

"She's not due for a couple more weeks, we've got time. Try not to worry about us. We really want to do this with him before we are too busy to go for a while. It's a lot harder when there's a little baby in the picture. Besides he really wants to go. We will be fine! Okay?"

I can tell she's not satisfied with my decision, but she says okay anyways.

Chance is surprisingly good at soccer. He scored two goals, and his best friend is on his team. After it was over we hit the beach as a family of three. It was a blast and no, our baby girl didn't come while we were away. She was a stubborn one and went two weeks over her due date. Weighing in at a heavy nine pounds, eight ounces.

"Daddy, Poppy is crying again. Tell momma to give sissy her boob so she quiets up."

Chance didn't see Meadow enter the room. I looked over at her and we both started laughing.

"He's a funny little shit, isn't he?"

"Shit... shit... shit..."

Meadow covers her mouth with her hands. Shocked that Chance is repeating a swear word. She points to me.

"This is all your fault. You fix it."

I shrug, pick Poppy up and kiss her chubby cheek. Then I handed her to Meadow.

"Hey buddy. What do you say we head out to the trees and finish our story?"

"Yes!"

Before I could catch up, Chance is out the back door and running towards the trees. We hung a swing up for him that he rides while I push him and I tell him stories that I totally make up on the fly. He doesn't seem to notice it's not from a book, but he always catches me when I make a mistake and get the back story wrong. He's the smartest kid I know.

Most of my stories are about second chances. I'm certain he doesn't catch on. But I tell them anyway. He will never know his story, I'm not sure he would fully understand it if we did tell him. Regardless, there's no reason for him to know. He's ours, that's *all* he needs to know.

He got a second chance at life when Emily... Meadow decided to run away that day over three years ago. The truth is, Meadow was everyone's second chance. One decision, one wild, reckless, completely beautiful decision that changed everything. She got on that bus that day with a baby that wasn't hers, and in doing so, she rerouted not just hers and Chances' lives, she changed four people's lives for the better. Forever. I guess that's the thing about second chances, they don't always come wrapped in logic. But when they do come, you'd be a fool not to take them. Meadow did, she took a huge chance... worth taking.

***

I read Meadow a poem last night after the kids fell asleep. Just the two of us, tangled beneath the Sycamores. A habit we never stopped, and we never will.

My poems have changed. We've changed. My words are now filled with hope and promises, not sadness and loss. We no longer live in sorrow. We live in love, in hope, in promise. This is where we were always meant to be.

I used to stand beneath these trees,
Alone with memories like falling leaves,
Falling slow, soft whispers gone,
A quiet place where I held on.

Then you came, and sowed our meadow,
A gentle field where our love will grow,

Lorinda Faye

A place of peace, bright sun, and soft rain,
Where broken hearts healed from their pain.

You were my chance, my open sky,
A breath of life. A whispered sigh,
And Chance, the child that was never planned,
The reason all this began.

His laughter stirs the ever-growing wildflowers,
His joy the light of long, bright hours,
A meadow blooming wild and free,
Where hope took root so tenderly.

Though loss once shadowed every day,
This love has found a softer way,
A chance worth taking, bold and true,
Four lives renewed, because of you.

Beneath these trees, beside the stream,
I hold this quiet and steady dream,
A family growing wild and strong,
Meadow's peace, where we all belong.

THE END.

Acknowledgements:

THANK YOU for taking a chance on this book. This is my second completed attempt from over three years' worth of passionately wanting to write every second of every day. This dream wasn't something I had dreamed of my entire life. I wasn't just born knowing I wanted to write. Writing just hit me one day, and I am so incredibly grateful for it. I have a lot to say and putting those words down in novels and other non-fiction pieces has turned into an obsession. I believe wholeheartedly that love is the answer for almost anything, so being able to share that with you all is very much appreciated. Thank you for coming on this journey with me. You are all an important part of this process for me.

I have a little more than a handful of people to thank for getting me to this second completed novel. Bear with me as I express my gratitude. If this sounds familiar it's because it's already perfect and still true today... so why change it?! :)

TO my kids who will always come first. Thank you, my loves, for supporting your mom on all her wild and continuously changing ideas and adventures. Sometimes we have a lot of fun with them and sometimes you must think I've lost my mind. Regardless, I hope I have taught you that you can do anything, you can change anything; any time you want. Please, please, please, follow your dreams! Take the risks! That's all I want for you. I'll be there rooting you on as your biggest fan. Love, Mom.

TO my mother and my stepfather for being my longest supporters.

Dana, you are my favorite person in this whole world! Growing up with you was my very own first version of Stroke of Luck. I'll never stop hearing the words "Heyyyyyy batter batter batter batter batter, saaa-wing batter!" in my head from Ferris Bueller's Day Off. Back then we were a great little duo! Well, this is me still swinging, hoping for a grand slam! You are my safe place to fall and my solid ground. I know you are proud of me always.

Mom, you said the most significant thing to me once when things got hard and it's something that has changed me and how I live. You said: "It's just money. There will be more." You never once blinked an eye when I needed you. You taught me a very important lesson that day when I needed it the most. It taught me that things will always get better, you just keep going, you keep trying. I've taken many chances on things because of that advice and here I am doing it again! This is me keeping it going.

I LOVE YOU BOTH SO MUCH!

TO my Gary. I thank all my lucky stars that you were there that day in that gym. I saw you from across the lobby and I knew I needed and wanted you and it has proven true again. I knew giving up on love wasn't an option for me and I feel like I won the ultimate prize for my patience. Please tell me I can keep you now!?

Lorinda Faye is a suspenseful romance author who blends heartfelt love stories with raw, emotional depth. Her debut, Stroke of Luck, captured readers with its mix of mystery, longing, and second-chance romance. With her newest release. Chance Worth Taking, she continues to explore love, healing, and the unexpected turns that shape our lives. She hopes you enjoy her work as much as she loves writing. She lives in Western New York with her five children, four dogs, two cats, and seven goats.

Connect with Lorinda.

Instagram @authorlorindafaye
Facebook @authorlorindafaye
TikTok @authorlorindafaye
Website: lorindafaye.com

Please Review! Indie Author's self-promote, and we rely on reviews to sell books. Please, please, please take the time to give a kind review! Amazon & Goodreads. THANK YOU SO MUCH!

A word from the author to other aspiring writers.

Write the book!

If it is your desire to write a book or write anything for that matter...

Just. Write. It!

Writing is hard. There's the intense worry and stress about editing, formatting, book covers and actually making the story line make any kind of sense. It takes so much time, self-doubt, and bravery. Then will anyone even like it!?! There's so much work that goes into just one book!

But...

You can do it! Don't worry about it being perfect. Don't stress if nobody likes it. (Someone will, a lot of someone's!)

If YOU like it that's enough!

My books probably have grammatical errors in it, more than I'd like to acknowledge. But I came to the decision that I don't really care. I wrote a damn book! A whole ass book!

And I self-published! What a huge and truly amazing accomplishment!

What if we set aside perfection and just GET CREATIVE and make that the whole point? I think we should, and I know I can't be the first to think so! I would read YOUR book that you're afraid to write and publish. I'd read your book even if it's not in perfect formation. I'd also read it with grammar errors! The point is to...

Just. Write. It!

(Then self- publish it.)

You've got this! I believe in YOU!